Terry Fox

Somewhere the Hurting Must Stop

a novel
by
John Passfield

Rock's Mills Press
Oakville, Ontario
2019

Published by
ROCK'S MILLS PRESS
www.rocksmillspress.com

For information, including Library and Archives Canada Cataloguing in Publication data, please contact us at customer.service@rocksmillspress.com.

Cover design: Craig Passfield
Cover photo: Jeremy Gilbert (Wikimedia Commons). While running across Canada during his Marathon of Hope, Terry insisted on wearing his blood-stained shorts even when meeting the Prime Minister and the Governor General, as he wanted everyone to see his prosthetic leg and the blood stains in order to emphasize what cancer does to people and how important it was to give money for cancer research.

Excerpts in each chapter from the article "Geological Regions" in *The Canadian Encyclopedia* are reproduced courtesy of *The Canadian Encyclopedia*, Historica Canada.

Author's website: www.johnpassfield.ca

Chapter 1

Dipping my leg in the Atlantic Ocean. Seagulls circling overhead. Muddy water, choppy currents, windy weather. April in St. John's, Newfoundland.

A boy with a missing leg.

This is where it all begins. The next time I dip my leg in the ocean I'll be back home. Atlantic to Pacific and every inch of road in between. The water is cold and muddy. Some construction going on. One of the water-jugs floats away. I want two jugs of seawater but I'm only going to get one. Weather report last night. A lot of bitter weather ahead. Did my training in BC so I'll be all right. Nice to have the cameras here. Newspaper people too. Hope everybody sees this. Gotta make sure everyone knows. Did a lot of phoning last night. Some of the towns seem very interested. Some of them don't seem to care. Wanted to start early this morning, but had to time this for maximum news. Reminding Doug to pass the bucket through the crowd. We're here for more than just photographs. Now it's off to a reception at City Hall.

Today.

A young boy telling a story in a cancer ward.
A Toyota slamming into the back of a truck.
A runner wearing a pair of bloody shorts.

Today is the day.

"Canada is a country which is bordered on the west by the Pacific Ocean, on the east by the Atlantic Ocean, on the south by the United States and on the north by the Arctic Ocean."

Today is the day it all begins.

What is the flame which burns within you?
What rage is hidden behind your eyes?
What dragons do you expect to be able to slay?

Running between St. John's and Portugal Cove. Tougher weather than I thought. Blowing snow and biting wind. It's April, but it feels like winter here.
A figure running along a windswept road.
Running along and thinking. Putting on the miles. I put everything in my life on hold. I left everything behind to go on this run – my parents, my brothers and sister. Just Doug, that's all I've brought from my life in BC. I'm not going to think about my life while I'm on the run. Not about school, not about a job, not about my future, not about Rika. Just the run, the publicity and the fund-raising – and that's all. I'll be thinking of cancer – nothing but cancer. Cancer can be beaten – Cancer can be beaten – Cancer can be beaten. That's all I'm going to think about while I'm running. That's all I'm going to talk about when I talk. I'll be living in the present, not the past. I left everything behind when I left BC. Whatever future I'll have can start when I get back.

"Behind me, a young Canadian, Terry Fox, from Port Coquitlam, British Columbia, is dipping his leg in the Atlantic Ocean, here, this morning, at St. John's, Newfoundland. It is the first act in what might well turn out to be the most gallant endeavor in Canadian history, as the young man's plan is to run from one end of Canada to the other, without missing an inch or a mile. Oh, and there is one other thing: the young man who plans to make this epic journey has only one leg."

"Nothing like this has been done before."
"Hard to say whether the kid is gonna make it."

"The term 'cancer' is applied to any of various malignant neoplasms which are characterized by the proliferation of anaplastic cells which tend to invade surrounding tissue and metastasize to new body sites. A cancerous state is the pathological condition which is characterized by such growths. In common parlance, the word 'cancer' is often used to signify a pernicious, spreading evil."

"I gave him my chain of office. Put it around his neck. I'm the mayor and I was wearing it at City Hall. I could tell it made him uneasy. I also gave him my robe. Draped it around his shoulders as he talked. Several times he made a gesture as he was talking into the microphone. He never spoke about it, but it was almost as if he was trying to shake it off. I suppose it was the jewelry. It's a pretty fancy chain. And the robe is made of velvet. And here he was talking about cancer and how all the money was going to be used to help the kids. The reason I think he didn't like what I did is that as soon as he finished speaking into the microphone he pulled the chain over his head and shrugged off the robe and gave them back to me. I didn't want to take over the proceedings. It was spontaneous on my part. I had a son who died of cancer and here was this young boy starting off on a cross-country run for cancer victims. It was almost as if he was my son. Without really thinking, I just gave him my chain and my robe."

A fisherman filleting a slew of cod.
Schoolchildren playing outside at recess.
Clapboard houses painted in bright colours.

Run through pain - distance from people - a big-enough story - as close as I can get - the force that is in your mind - plate-tectonic process- always coming towards us - pain is always there - a trillion years, infinity - osteogenic sarcoma.

I wasn't born in British Columbia. I was born in Winnipeg. That's almost half-way across Canada from BC.

Mom grew up on a farm. Dad was a switchman on the railway. They met in Winnipeg and married and settled down.

All of us were born in Manitoba. Fred and me and Daryll and Judith. Four kids, two parents – seems about what a family should be.

"I want the foundation to be extra-strong," the man said.
"I want it to keep the fires of hell from burning our feet."

Running between Clarenville and Port Blandford. Standing beside the van. Cold wind whipping along the highway. Shivering in the cold.

A runner whose breath makes a cloud in the biting wind.

Why can't he find a sock? All I need is one dry sock. I've got to talk to Doug. It's not enough just to drive the van. He should be setting aside some socks the night before. That's all he has to do. Why is that so hard? He was joking around in the laundry room but he wasn't doing his job. Easy for him to search for a sock in the van with the heater going full blast while I stand out on the highway dripping with sweat in the bone-chilling wind and wait for a sock. I knew I should have brought Darrell. Too bad he had to stay for exams. This wind is getting colder. It's whipping right along. I'm going to get pneumonia and have to give up the run. And all because Doug can't find a bloody sock!

"The young man who is running behind me, here, on the Trans-Canada highway, about a quarter of the way across Newfoundland, is Terry Fox. He is determined to run clear across Canada – a distance of over five thousand miles – before the winter sets in. He stops at town halls and schools to talk about his experiences, in losing his leg and in finding a way to contribute to the fight against the disease that tried, and failed, to cripple him. In every speech, Terry mentions the young sufferers whom he has had to leave behind, but has not forgotten, in the cancer ward. It is for these young people – and their future – that he conceived of the Marathon of Hope."

Drawing lines on a map of the Trans-Canada highway.
Planning to run two hundred marathons in a row.

Snow slashing my face as I climb a slippery hill.
A cancer organizer explaining that the run is a big mistake.
A messenger coming to a runner in a dream.

"We were riding on the school bus. Heading home from school. It was just another day. Heading home to do your homework and hit the chores. And everybody's chatting or slumping down. Not much happening. Then somebody says, 'Hey, there's that guy from the news!' So everybody perks up and starts to look. 'The boy who's running for cancer!' So we all stand up in the aisle and open the windows and peer out the side. And there he is! Just a guy on one leg and a pair of shorts with an artificial limb. Moving along stride by stride. And it hit me that he was going to do this all across Canada. And here he was on one of our back-country roads. These roads are agony for us if we miss the school bus. Your bag of books after a full day at school. Hoping for a pickup truck to give you a ride. And he was on his way to British Columbia. We all turned and shuffled to the back of the bus. All crammed in the aisle and on the seats and staring out the back window at this guy. The school bus bouncing along over the ruts. And pretty soon we had left him far behind."

A man biting off a chew of tobacco.
A white church in a rocky cove.
A pile of kindling stacked beside a stove.

"He's the boy from Port Coquitlam."
"He's the boy from British Columbia."

Think at the top of your mind - an undifferentiated mass - front-page news - what is the value - allow myself to dream - all the demons in hell - what could one wish for - the last thing you would want - make you disable yourself - feeling very, very alone.

I had a nice childhood in Manitoba. Colouring at school; riding my trike; running through the sprinkler in the back yard. Then, all of sudden, we were told we were moving away.

My parents decided to move to the coast. Left some relatives behind. Dad said he was starting to think of Manitoba as just too cold.

I spent my youth in Port Coquitlam, British Columbia. That's about seventeen miles from Vancouver. About as good a place as any for someone to be.

A man was returning from the oracle.
Trying hard to remember what the sage had said.

Running through Gambo. The coughing comes and goes. Always the pain, but I keep it under control.

A young man giving a speech on a cold day.

Gambo is great. What a reception. Everybody in the town is here today. A man is waving twenty dollars. A worried look in his face. Worried that Doug will pass by the crowd before he can put his money in the bucket. Cancer can be licked. I will never take a dollar for my own use. It would spoil it for everybody – especially for me. I wave at the man as I run past him but he's looking at the bucket and doesn't see me wave.

"Canada is the second-largest country in the world, by land mass, exceeded in size only by the vast expanse of Russia."

What is it that makes you think that you can do this?
What are the qualities that you will draw on for this ordeal?
Do you realize that people on two legs have tried and failed?

"Phidippides was running. From Athens to Sparta this time. Leather pouch with a water-bottle; sandal-leather pounding the path. Bandana around his head to combat the sun. He was what was called a runner. A soldier whose role it was to run messages to all the far-flung corners of ancient Greece."

St. John's - Portugal Cove - St. Phillip's - Paradise - Mt. Pearl - Mahers - Ocean Pond - Whitbourne - Chapel Arm - Belleview - Chance Cove - Arnold's Lane - Come by Chance - Goobies - North West Brook - Adeytown - Clarenville - Port Blandford - Charlottetown - Glovertown - Gambo - Benton - Gander - Minchy - Glenwood - Note Dame Junction - Norris Arm - Bishop's Falls - Grand Falls-Windsor.

"In the twenty-five days of his challenging run across the entire length of Newfoundland, Terry Fox has compiled a total of five hundred and seventy-six miles of what he is calling 'The Marathon of Hope for Cancer Research.' "

"Hello there. It's a long time since I've seen you. Actually, I'm just heading out for my Saturday morning jog."

Running between Gander and Minchy. Wiping the tears away with my shirt-sleeve and plunging ahead.
An exhausted person stretched out on a bed.
April in Newfoundland. Blowing snow and freezing temperatures. Butting up against the wind. What's the difference between Gambo and Gander? That's the question I asked Doug last night as we ate our hamburgs. One day the whole village comes out to the fire hall and there's speeches and smiles and photographs. The next day you go to a town and there's just the mayor and a couple of councillors and a tiny cheque. The hills get steeper when I'm disappointed. The wind gets colder when the people don't care. I'm putting everything into my running. I'm hollowed out at the end of each day. Doug tells me I should do all the phoning. He says nobody wants to talk to him. Says they all want to talk to the star. I need another Terry Fox to go ahead of me and tell them I'm coming to town.

"We have set up our camera here on the Trans-Canada highway about three quarters of the way across the province of Newfoundland. Terry Fox is doing what he does best: running, inch by inch, and mile by mile, along the Trans-Canada highway. In the next town – one of thousands through which Terry will run in his epic adventure – crowds are waiting to greet the intrepid runner, and to donate to the cause. Terry is asking that every Canadian donate one dollar to cancer research, an act which, if realized, would raise over twenty-four million dollars for the fight against this dread disease."

"You know, the kid really shouldn't be running."
"Hard to believe that stump will hold up for five thousand miles."

Kids playing road hockey in the street.
Getting the silent treatment from Doug.
Deciding to wear my shorts no matter how cold it gets.

"Just think of the audacity of it all. You hear about these athletes running a marathon – twenty-six miles – and they're feeding them cups of water and they're collapsing from the heat and passing out and people are helping them to the finish-line and they're carrying them off on stretchers, and then here's this crazy kid from BC asking for donations and telling all these people he's going to run a marathon a day. On one leg he's going to do this? He's asking for a camper van and hotel rooms and groceries and running shoes and all the things he figures he's going to need. And so people are receiving these letters and admiring the kid's intentions and wondering how many days or weeks – at the most – he's going to last. And the people back in BC – the people close to Terry – sure they know his strength of mind – but they must be wondering what it will do to him – how devastating it'll be – if he has to drop out. But there was something inside him that brought everybody along."

A lighthouse on a bluff against the sky.
A girl reading a book in a library.
Houses clinging to a rocky hillside.

Alone with his thoughts - in constant pain - work on your strengths - errors in the instructions - little girl who cried - keep the pain away - no chance of appeal - the only one who knows - an angle and the truth - filling the bucket with donations.

I liked Geography as a subject. There were maps at the back of the book. You could trace your finger across the page as you dreamed.

Port Coquitlam is in British Columbia. BC is part of Canada. Canada is part of the world.

I always thought I'd like to see all of Canada someday. I already knew about Manitoba. Hoped to tour all of Canada and come right back home to BC.

The hare prayed to the god of the forest.
"Make me as swift as the tortoise in tomorrow's race."

Running between Grand Falls and Windsor. Seeing double. Glassy eyes. Light-headed. Running through it all. No way I'll give it up.

Children in snow suits crowding around a boy wearing shorts.

These school kids are just the best. Standing in the foyer. Kids crammed in from wall to wall. Singing at the top of their voices. Thank you Lord for giving us Terry! The teachers are all singing too. Pulling myself up to attention. Tears clouding up my eyes. They're donating their recess money. All of the agony is suspended. This is the reason I'm doing this run. It's the kids who understand me. They know what I'm all about. Let the kids just keep on singing. How am I going to talk after this? What am I going to do with these tears? I don't even have a hanky to wipe my face.

"Just down the road, in the distance, Terry Fox is approaching our cameras in his deliberate, determined way. It is safe to say now, with so many miles behind him, as he makes his dash across Newfoundland, that the Marathon of Hope is in good shape and even thriving. The young man who is making this epic journey is raising funds for cancer research, in hopes that young people, in future, who are stricken by this disease, will have an even better chance at a normal life than he, himself, has had."

Rolling out of bed at four AM.
Worrying about my enlarged heart.

Learning to talk in front of people.
A cheque for ten thousand dollars from Port aux Basques.
Making the school kids run as fast as they can.

"The problem was that nobody had ever heard of him. Sure he got a minute or two on national TV but that didn't amount to much. That's just a bit of novelty to lighten the news. So you get a call saying that so and so's running across Canada and he's going to be in your town tomorrow or a week away and can you help him raise some funds for cancer research? And you're thinking – we've already had our annual drive for cancer research. That's when all our volunteers go all out to raise awareness and spread the word to the community. Now they're all played out. And the donors are all tapped out too. So what do you do when you get that phone call? Well, you scrabble a few people together – the mayor and the local press – and try to come up with a few donors and a modest cheque for a presentation. Sure I met him and shook his hand and I could see that his heart was in the right place. But to organize a fund-raising drive – he didn't have a clue. He was just a kid with a dream and not much else. A thing like this you gotta plan at least a year in advance. You don't just phone up people and say you're coming to town. Heart as big as the world and all but the timing was just not right for this one-legged kid."

Two old fellows playing checkers on a barrel.
Fishing dories knocking against the dock.
A Canadian flag swinging lazily in the breeze.

"He's the boy from all of Canada."
"There's a kid like him in every neighbourhood."

Other terry foxes - uncontrolled growth - time for my future - exactly what i am - a few drops of blood - tested to the maximum - being eaten alive - they don't add up - others will be here - riding in a fire truck - bad luck swallowing good luck.

Hockey holds Canada together. Hockey and football on TV. Two of my heroes are Daryll Sittler and Bobby Orr.
I loved playing hockey on the out-door rink. We always got lots of winter in BC. Shovelled the rink during the Christmas holidays and played all day.

Loved the hockey game I got for Christmas. Challenged everybody to play. Invited the neighbourhood kids in and trounced them game after game.

A pygmy found himself in the presence of a giant.
The giant didn't notice that the pygmy was there.

Running between Steady Brook and Corner Brook. Raw and bleeding stump. Keeping it out of my thoughts. Eyes on the road. Enough of a wave to let them know I hear. Can't stop where there's clusters of people. When I get to a spot that's bare, I'll take a break.

A small group of people huddling on a country road.

I'm not going to get that x-ray. Not when I get to Corner Brook. I'm not going to let them have a look. The Cancer Society's getting cold feet. They're afraid I'm going to croak. Well, they can book all the x-rays they want to but I'm not going to cooperate. They're afraid I'm going to drop dead and then where would they be? They want to pull me off the road to avoid embarrassment. Well I'm testing my heart every day. Get your feet down off the desk and get your running shoes on. Get out here and run beside me if you want to know if I'm going to make it. Ask those school kids I talk to about my heart.

"A number is born to be a servant," the ring-master said.
"A number's greatest wish is to simply obey."

People inviting us into their homes for a bath and a meal.
A guru and an acolyte having a talk.
A reporter in a big winter coat and a toque.

"Just sign the contract – first things first.
Any adjustments can be improvised as we go."

"Anyone wishing to appreciate the wide diversity of the Canadian land-scape is advised to traverse its vast distances by means of the train."

Fires burning; desolate landscape.
No bird would dare to sing.

Can you handle the physical requirements?
Can you handle the mental requirements?
What factors will be entirely out of your control?

A motel room in Port aux Basques. Lying on the bed. My last night in Newfoundland.

A figure in the flickering light of a TV screen.

Ferry trip in the morning to Nova Scotia. Fish and chips tonight to celebrate. TV on with no sound. News – news – news. Fighting in the Middle East – Russia and the United States – Speeches from the United Nations. Weather for the week ahead. What to think about Newfoundland? I've been running for twenty-five days. Been running across a whole province. One down and nine to go. Artificial leg and stump are holding up. Some days beautiful, some days brutal. Sun and wind and sights that take my breath away. Fishing villages that look like a painting from out of a book. Days that bring me down, days that lift me up. The school kids are always the ones that make it worthwhile. Collecting a lot of money, but not enough. Hoping for a dollar from every Canadian. We need a lot more publicity. Fund-raising has to pick up speed. Choppy weather tomorrow it says on the news. Hope I don't get sick on the ferry ride.

Chapter 2

Great to be in Nova Scotia. Between Sydney Mines and Big Bras d'Or. Four-thirty AM. Silence in the van. No music. No one speaks. Poking along in the dark.

Two faces in the glow of dashboard lights.

Doug looking for a pile of stones that he made to mark the last run. Moonlight, rows of fences, cattle in the fields. Why doesn't Doug figure out a better method of finding yesterday's spot? Never mind. Never mind. Got to keep myself from exploding. Just let it all flow over me. Always better to run in the mornings. Like to put on as many miles as I can in the dark. Get the bulk of the running done before it's noon. Never know what it's going to be like in the afternoons.

A marathon a day.

Camping on a hill in Nova Scotia.
The pain of down-hill jogs.
Wondering why Doug doesn't just leave.

A marathon a day clear across Canada.

"Based on geological history, Canada can be divided into six regions, each characterized by a distinctive landscape: the Canadian Shield, Interior Platform, Appalachian Orogen, Innuitian Orogen, Cordillera and Western Canada

Sedimentary Basin, and the Eastern Continental Margin."

The second-largest country in the world.

Why should people pay attention?
Why should people give a moment's thought to cancer?
Why should the cries of the children be echoing in their ears?

Running between Auld's Cove and Havre Boucher. Rain and hail-stones in the morning. Blistering sun in the afternoon.
A person running with an artificial leg.
It might not look like running to some, but I'm going as hard as I can. It's not a walk and it not a trot. It's as close as I can get to a two-legged run. I always correct people when they congratulate me on my walk. I've always been competitive. I turn it on when people join me in the run. They think they'll jog along beside me, but I always make 'em sweat. It's not a walk around the park. It's a marathon a day. Be prepared to grunt and sweat as you grind out the miles. Run a mile or two with me and you'll know it's a run.

"The runner behind me, on this lonely stretch of highway, is Terry Fox, who is here in Nova Scotia – his run across Newfoundland now behind him – on what might be called the second leg of his attempt to run clear across Canada in an effort to raise awareness – and much-needed funds – for cancer research."

"The kid's got a lot more in him than a lot of people realize."
"If anyone can do it, Terry Fox is your man."

"A simple definition of cancer is that it is a serious disease which is caused by cells which are not normal and can spread to one or many parts of the body. It means something bad or dangerous which causes other bad things to happen."

"We sat in a stairwell. Just Terry and I. A quiet moment. We were waiting for the kids to file into the gym. He seemed a little nervous. Told me he'd hardly ever spoken in public before. He said he'd like to tell them what it's like to get cancer. And how it was the kids who suffer the most. They were the ones with so much to live for. And the fund-raising. He didn't want to forget and leave that out. 'But I don't want it to be boring. Not like a lecture – not like that.' So I said 'Why not talk about your leg? How it works and how you walk? How you can manage to run and things like that?' A cloud faded away and his face lit up. 'That's it! That what I'll show them! I can tell them I only need half as many socks!' I could tell that he'd been worried. Now all I saw was that ear-to-ear Terry Fox smile."

Fishing nets drying in the sunshine.
A village built on stilts on the edge of a cliff.
Waves crashing against a rocky shore.

Reach a meaningful milestone - a buzz-saw - always pretty focused - a process called subduction - turning into skeletons - people I admire - what is the connection - hugging my parents - tall trees reaching forever - dizziness, double-vision - the numbers keep going up.

Dad never said much, but you always knew what he was thinking. The law was the law and you always knew what it meant. There was never an inch of leeway when Dad made a rule.

Mom was the one to think things over. "First let's talk about it and figure out what to do." Always better to talk to Mom before you'd decide.

There were four of us kids in the family. People said we fought like cats and dogs. But let anyone come between us and they'd find out what family means.

"I want the roof to be extra-strong," the man said.
"I want it to keep the cares of heaven from pressing us down."

Running between Salt Springs and Lochaber. Some people flinch at the blood on my shorts but that's the point. Give me a few extra dollars if you feel my pain. This isn't a movie of a run – it's a real run.

A person flipping the pages of a book.

Beautiful scenery and better weather. Temperatures warming up but still very cold. I've read a lot of those running manuals. – There is no bad weather; only bad preparation. – Always dress appropriately. Well, I'm running in my shorts no matter what. Rain, snow, sleet – I just don't care. I want everybody to see my artificial leg. I want everybody to know what cancer does. It's being eaten by a shark every day. I don't care if get pneumonia. I'm all I've got to show. I want everybody to see what cancer does so they'll want to give their money and find a cure. I'm running in my shorts no matter what the weather throws at me from here on in.

"Just to put this whole enterprise in perspective for you, the ancient Greek runner, Phidippides, ran for twenty-six miles just once, and he is reported to have dropped dead of exhaustion at the end of his run. Phidippides ran twenty-six miles that fateful day, which became the standard for the Marathon. And now, this young Canadian – Terry Fox – is determined to run a marathon a day – from the Atlantic to the Pacific – clear across the extremely challenging landscape of Canada."

Writing in my journal.
Checking my favourite sock.

Making my own lunch and getting my own water.
Crying over the phone to my mom and my dad.
Listening to people tell their cancer stories.

"He leaned over and kissed me. We were standing in the gym. It was a different kind of Terry than I saw on the run. He gave his speech and then the kids all crowded around him. I found myself alone with him in the crowd. I told him my dad had died a year before. I just blurted it out without thinking. How he died of lung cancer and his death was terribly hard. How my mom has never recovered from our loss. Then he just leaned over and kissed me on the cheek. He didn't say a word. He didn't have to. Then he chatted with the other kids and we all went out on the run. The other Terry was the one who ran ahead of us. He really turned it on. Wasn't going to let a bunch of kids get ahead of him. I saw him run on TV every time they did those news reports. He always looked so grim when he ran. I knew there was another Terry inside."

A man rocking in a chair on a wooden porch.
Seagulls dipping and diving behind a ferry.
A sailing vessel tied up at a dock.

"Curly-headed, good-looking and sun-tanned."
"An athlete of amazing endurance and strength."

Raise their game - gets in a groove - haunts your thoughts - turned a corner - athens is saved - the story of cinderella - birds singing at sunrise - looking for a pile of stones - a ring master controlling - people taking us home - trapped in a well.

Every one of us Foxes was stubborn, for sure. Argue over everything and never, ever give up. In the Fox family, you learned to stick up for yourself.

Dad and Mom taught us a lot. Work hard at what you do. Never quit what you start.

Give your word and make sure you keep it. Earn your own money as soon as you can. Stick up for your family because they're the best thing that you've got.

"Good luck will swallow bad luck."
Is this what the oracle foretold?

Running between Goldenville and Liscomb. My thigh is freezing with the cold, but I won't wear sweats. I want everybody along the route to see my legs.

A person running beside a snowdrift wearing shorts.

Giving speeches everywhere. Telling everybody how much I like Nova Scotia. The beautiful valleys, the fishing villages, the rock and the water and the trees. Very few dogs or trucks or traffic. Friendly people everywhere. Thanking the kids for their contributions. Thanks for running along beside me. Setting a pretty good pace. Always like to make these runners test themselves.

"The North American continent, of which Canada represents the northern half, was assembled from continental fragments by the process of plate tectonics."

Why should people look ahead to woeful times?
Why should they dwell on the worst until it happens?
Shouldn't cancer be the furthest thing from their minds?

"It was hot and Phidippides was exhausted. His water-bottle gave out too soon. A high-speed run across the landscape of ancient Greece was a brutal undertaking. The sun beat down; the creeks were dry; he barked his shins on the sharpest rocks. He couldn't allow himself to take the needed rest. He was the messenger and the message had to get through."

Badger - South Brook - Sheppardville - Reidville - Deer Lake - Pynn's Brook - Pasadena - Little Rapids - Steady Brook - Corner Brook - George's Lake - Barachois Brook - South Branch – Benoit's Siding - Doyles - Red Rocks - Cape Ray - Port aux Basques - Sydney - North Sydney - Sydney Mines - Big Bras d'Or - Englishtown - Baddeck - Hunter's Mountain - Bucklaw - Whycomagh.

"While here, in Nova Scotia, Terry Fox has run three hundred and ninety-six miles in sixteen days for a cross-Canada total which has now reached nine hundred and seventy-two miles."

"Believe it or not, it's my birthday today. I'm fifty years old. Who can believe that time goes by so fast?"

Running between Spry Bay and Popes Harbour. Fifteen pushups along the road-side. Clearing away the cobwebs and the double-sight.

A young man talking to a patient in a hospital bed.

Some of these places have never heard of me. People gawk at me on the street as I run along. That's the thing that pulls me down. Have to get on the phone every night and try to scare up some interest in every town. Then the accident with the TV crew. They were taping me from the door of the van when the truck came over the hill. Truck didn't even slow down. Couldn't run any more that day. Thank God they'll be all right. They were cheerful enough in the hospital. Nice to visit them and all. I've been in lots of hospitals, but every time I go I get the same thoughts. Today I'm catching up on the miles. I'll keep going as long as I can today. Why quit early when all I've got is Doug and the phone?

"There is some doubt that all is well in the Terry Fox camp, as the tensions that have been simmering have reached boiling proportions. The rigours of the run and the somewhat disappointing returns in terms of raising funds for cancer research have sometimes meant that the optimism – so important for such an endeavour – has been hard to find."

"He ran three thousand miles as preparation."
"If it's a contest I wouldn't bet against Terry Fox."

A lobster dinner with a bunch of firemen.
Filling out postcards for Doug to mail.
Learning to guard myself with the media.

"You could tell that he was getting frustrated. He didn't say much but he didn't contradict what some others said. He was very diplomatic because the cameras were there and a few reporters even had their tape recorders. He would nod and say something general, like 'There's a lot of potential in this run. There's a lot of people who would give if they knew about me.' Others were being a lot more blunt. 'The Cancer Society is missing the boat.' 'They better get on the bandwagon.' 'They're missing out.' The frustration showed on his face. You could tell he was aware of the media. Wanted to be careful to say the right words. I couldn't say they were trying to goad him. They just kept asking him how the donations were going. And if the Cancer Society was doing all it could. He just kept talking about the potential. How important it was to inspire people. How he wanted to send out the message. How the kids were living in pain. You could tell he felt some frustration. He was learning to let others say what he shouldn't say."

Kids selling scallops along the roadside.
An old sea captain with watery eyes.
A road wandering for miles along the seashore.

Perfect weather, perfect scenery, perfect day - troubles of the world - managing his life - bored right into your brain - dead dreams - to do with helping kids - as bad as things can get - a young boy fishing - cuts like a knife to the heart - get a free ride.

Get your two cents in if you know you're right. Keep your mouth shut if you're wrong. And don't forget that your parents are always the boss.

Stay out of trouble. Keep your nose clean. Don't forget to clean up your room.

Don't whine about things you can change. Don't change things without knowing why. And don't ever forget you're a Fox and you know who you are.

The tortoise prayed to the god of the forest.
"Make me as swift as the hare in tomorrow's race."

Running between East Preston and Loon Lake. Twenty-eight miles today. Not bad. Not bad at all.

Two people arguing angrily at a country cross-roads.

I think Doug is getting tired of it. But I can't let Doug affect me. Some people find it hard to accept a routine. He sits in the van all day. – Inching along the road. – Stopping every mile. – Getting me a drink. – Finding me a dry sock. – Listening to the same old songs. – Thinking whatever he thinks. Mile by mile. Hour by hour. Day by day. For him it's a rut. For me it's a groove. His mood is getting sour. So I'm stuck with Doug and Doug is stuck with me. Every day is just the same. – We argue over something. – We're silent for a while. – We argue again. I don't know what to do. Doug is poisoning my mood. I can't allow Doug to drain my hope away.

"Terry Fox's parents have flown here to Nova Scotia from British Columbia to visit their son, amid rumours that all is not well in the Terry Fox camp. There has been some speculation that the young man who is running across Canada in order to raise funds for cancer research is not happy with the way that the run is being organized."

Sleeping in a parking lot.
Washing my face in a creek.

Eating supper with the ocean sparkling down below.
Throwing a cup of water in Doug's face.
Wearing my shorts in freezing weather.

"We all sat down for a lobster dinner. Hey, what else are you going to eat out here? His parents flew in to visit him. I guess he was feeling pretty low. They were trying to cheer him up. The publicity was pretty spotty. The fund-raising was not going well. Most of us were firemen. The guys at the station arranged the meal. About ten of us or so. And he was so glad to be with his parents. Somehow it just all came out. Both his parents looked around the table as if to wonder if any of us was going to tell tales. Well, of course, we'd keep his secrets. They sized us up pretty fast. But anyway, they couldn't have stopped him. It was a pot that was boiling over. How there wasn't much publicity. How the donations were pretty small. How there was anger in the van. How he was busting his hump and not getting a heck of a lot back. Anyway, they let him talk it all out. We were all eating lobster all this time. Then one of his parents says to Terry 'Be disappointed but don't be mad'. He seemed to think this was good advice. Anyways, it didn't spoil his appetite."

A school bell ringing as the kids come out to play.
Church suppers with all you can eat.
A teenager waxing a car beside a house.

"He makes you think twice about labelling people as disabled."
"He's expanding the limits of what an amputee can do."

Plunged right into life - i'm just terry fox - to pay the price - two of terry fox - the cares of heaven - can't let that be the run - using a bullhorn - the high school basketball team - a nagging fear.

I was always crazy about sports. People would ask me why I took things to such an extreme. I'd shrug and tell them I guess I just like to compete.

Some sports I liked better than others. I liked cross-country running and basketball, one-on-one. Any sport that helped you find out what you're made of inside.

Cross-country running was really grueling. Covered in mud and fighting the heaves. At the end the coach always waiting to slap our hands and call out "Way to go, men".

The pygmy knew that he could not ignore the giant.
The giant was enormous in every way.

Running between Shubanacadie and Stewiake. Cheeseburger, apple pie and a milkshake. That's all I'm thinking about.
An alarm-clock lighting a silhouette on a bed.
I've always ignored everything I felt was going to interfere. I ignored the snickers of the basketball players when I first went out for the team. I ignored my sore knee when I bumped it on the dashboard of my car. I ignored Rika when I thought she was getting serious about us. I ignored how hard it was to run on a artificial limb. I ignored the size of Canada when I first started to think about this run. Now I'm ignoring the doctors who tell me I need a rest. I'm ignoring the pain in my hip and my knee and my ankle. I'm ignoring how comfortable the sleeping bag is when the alarm goes off at four-thirty in the morning. Maybe cancer is tracking me down. I don't believe it is, but if it is then it's the thing I've

got to ignore.

"The seconds, the minutes, the hours – the days, the weeks, the years.
They form up in sixties, twenty-fours, sevens and fifty-twos."

Calling the cancer society in the evenings.
Feeling very, very alone.
Fire engines and a police escort at Spring Hill.

"Sunshine for both in the morning; rain for both of us at night.
A partnership of equals, you and I."

"Scientists think that this process started more than three billion years ago, when the production of continental crust first began."

Swept by a hurricane?
Swamped by a flood?

Do people see death when they look at you?
Are you a reminder of blood and bone?
Are you a reminder of just how threatened our lives actually are?

Lying in the van. Between Springhill and Amherst. Hope I get to fall asleep. Looking forward to Prince Edward Island.
A person lying down with eyes wide open.
Thinking over the goods and bads of Nova Scotia. Wonderful people. Beautiful scenery. Some very generous donations but not enough publicity. What to do to get out the word? How can I make everybody know what cancer does? Everybody is just like me. I never thought about cancer until it came and got me. Got to make everybody aware of the suffering kids.

Chapter 3

Running, running, running. Good to be here in Prince Edward Island.
A young man talking earnestly in a phone booth.
Staying in motels and camping in church parking lots or along the road-side in the country. Phoning from pay-phones for a little publicity – maybe an article in the local newspaper or at least a mention on local TV. Some of them think it's just a hoax or not really newsworthy. Running for cancer doesn't seem to some people to be news. One reporter told me that her editor said that one mention is enough. A few more miles and a few more dollars isn't a big-enough story to print. He told her it won't be news again until I stop.

I know it isn't going to be easy.

Riding with the ferry-boat captain.
A radio reporter outside our door at five AM.
Getting lean and in the groove.

I know it's going to be very hard.

"During the Hadean period, early Earth consisted of an undifferentiated mass of largely molten matter which was created by the buildup of materials in the form of planetismals and meteorites circling around the sun in the primitive solar system."

The price that I pay is running in constant pain.

Five o'clock in the dark with a bitter wind in your face?
A pair of headlights on the pavement as the rain beats down hard?
Ever get the feeling that you're doing this all alone?

Running between Borden-Carlton and Tryon. Still freezing but wearing my shorts so people can see my leg.
Ocean spray drenching a runner from head to foot.
I do all my thinking when I run. When I'm off, I want to have a hollow head. I need everything around me to be as empty-headed as possible. Whatever is on TV. Cartoons, game shows, wrestling. Moving wallpaper with sound. Anything to fill up the room that isn't news. Just mindless stuff that's playing on the TV.

"As he runs behind me here, occasionally dodging traffic, towards Charlottetown, Prince Edward Island, Terry Fox enters the third phase of his Marathon of Hope. In his efforts to raise awareness about the need for cancer research, Terry has run successfully across the length of two of the Canadian provinces."

"Pretty brutal out there at five o'clock in the morning."
"Have to admit, I thought he'd probably quit and go home."

"Cancer is not just one disease, but a large group of almost one hundred diseases. Its two main characteristics are uncontrolled growth of the cells in the human body and the ability of these cells to migrate from the original site and spread to distant sites. If the spread is not controlled, cancer can result in death."

"I'd left the cancer ward for the day. Just one day. I was glad my son could take the day off work. I didn't want him to. I told him it isn't necessary but he insisted. 'Dad, I'm not letting you do this alone.' I tried to find out what time Terry would be running along the street but nobody seemed to know. 'Depends when he gets here' they said. My son kept asking me if I wanted to go sit down. 'There's a restaurant near the corner.' 'No way,' I kept saying. 'I don't want to miss him. I don't know how close he'll be. He'll probably run down the middle of the street. They block the streets off when he runs on the TV.' I had nothing I needed to say to him. I didn't even plan to call out. I don't have much of a voice anymore anyway. I just wanted to swell the throng. Saw it on TV that he had some thin crowds when he started out. Just wanted to help to fill up the sidewalk as he ran by. He knows cancer; I know cancer. No need to shout out or have a talk. He would know what I was thinking by just my being there."

An old fellow planing a plank for a fishing skiff.
Kids playing games outside a school.

Waves on a windy day pounding the seashore.

Focus on everything - squashing us flat - a tiny figure running - try to be the best - come to the window - meaning for everyone - first and final words - take myself to the limit - tumbling through his mind - one or more specialists.

Played a lot of basketball. Two guys snickered when I first went out to play. I looked around and everyone there was taller than me.

I could never seem to score. That's what made me get up early for practice. I ran from my house to the high school in the dark.

I was a buzz-saw on that court. Wiped the snickers off their faces. If I couldn't score in basketball, I could force those other guys to raise their game.

"I want the walls to be extra-strong," the man said.
"I want it to keep the troubles of the world from squashing us flat."

Running between Crapaud and Victoria. Clusters of people at country cross-roads. People coming out to support me and cheer me on.

Two people riding silently in a van.

I know I'm really tough on Doug. I bring my moods in off the road with me. But when I think about it, what else can I do? It would be nice if I could do everything myself. Just Terry Fox doing everything as he runs along the roads. Driving the van, having the water ready, checking the mileage, finding a sock, phoning ahead in the evenings to make some plans. It would be nice if I was two people – the runner and somebody else. Then my moods wouldn't bother anybody but me.

"A number of questions are being asked about the Marathon of Hope, which is being run by the young British Columbia amputee. Chief among them is whether he will have the physical stamina to endure the gruelling summer run across the sheer expanse of the vast Canadian landscape."

Expecting to reach home by early December.
Seeing double and wiping my eyes.

Fending off questions about my weight.
A path with sharp rocks and desert sands.
Sitting down to a seafood dinner with mom and dad.

"I was standing in a crowd. In front of the Canadian Tire Store. On the sidewalk. I kept inching to the front. I'm not very tall and I didn't want to let anybody stand in front of me. They talked about how a whole bunch of people were going to run with him. The mayor and people like that. So I started to worry that maybe I wouldn't get to see him. What if he's surrounded and I can't see? Then everybody got quiet and we all just stood and watched. A police cruiser with a flashing light. Then Terry Fox all by himself. It was painful to see that artificial leg. It should have looked awkward but he made it seem very graceful. He didn't smile. More like a determined frown. You just knew he was going to make it. It was all right there on his face. Clear across Canada. Nothing was going to stop him. That was the look on his face. There was a crowd of runners close behind him. We all burst out into clapping. There were people collecting with buckets. It all went by very quickly and then he was gone."

A woman covered with flour up to the elbows.
Couples dancing reels to an old-time fiddler.
Stinging sand whipping across a beach.

"He's a beacon to anyone who is lost at sea."
"He makes us believe in the human race again."

Meteors flashing at night - bus driver collecting money - vast canadian landscape - told his story - caught the imagination - double-good news - as clear as a pane of glass - lights blink in the ward - die before i quit - the ghost who looks like a person.

I guess it was me against myself. No matter who was in front of me when I was playing in a game. The guy I tried so hard to beat was always me.

So I played a lot of sports. The thing that I liked was to try to overcome big odds. Whatever looked too hard I wanted to try.

Long distance running. Setting new goals. Running past a series of barriers of pain.

"Bad luck will swallow good luck."
Is this what the oracle foretold?

Running between South Melville and Bonshaw. Doug handed me my sweats and I threw them back in the van. How many times have I told him I want them to see my legs?

A shiny water bucket filled with cash.

There's no in-between with me. I'm competitive. – I'm a dreamer. – I like challenges. – I don't give up. When I think of something I do it. And I always go all out. As soon as I thought of this run – to run a marathon a day – all the way across Canada – from coast to coast – with every Canadian giving a dollar for cancer research – I knew that I wouldn't stop 'til I'd made the run. Wouldn't matter what was against me. Wouldn't matter who gave me advice. Wouldn't matter what the doctors would say. Or who would give help or who would get in the way. As soon as I had the idea I knew I would run.

"Under the force of gravity, the lighter elements gradually migrated towards the Earth's surface and it was this process that began the differentiation of the Earth's surface into continental and oceanic crust."

Did you know that there might be rain-storms?
Did you know there'd be sleet and hail?
Did you think you would run in sunshine day after day?

"Phidippides wiped his brow without slowing his pace. Dripping sweat and feeling faint. All he could think of was the message. The Persians were threatening Greece. The Athenians were facing the brunt of the massive attack. The commander was blunt and anxious. 'Take a message to the Spartans. We are few! The Persians loom! Greece is at stake! There is little time to lose. Tell them we'll hold the Persians off for as long as we can.' "

Blues Mills - Melford - Glendale - Port Hastings - Port Hawksbury - Auld's Cove - Havre Boucher - Linwood - Trocadie - Heatherton - Antigonish - Salt Springs - Lochaber - College Grant - Stillwater - Sherbrooke - Goldenville - Liscomb - Liscomb Mills - Ecum Secum - Moser River - Moosehead - West Quaddy - Port Dufferin - Beaver Harbour - Watt Section - Sheet Harbour - Mushaboom - Spry Bay - Popes Harbour - Tangier - Murphy Cove.

"Terry Fox's three days in Prince Edward Island have added seventy-one miles to his run for a grand total of one thousand and seventy-four miles."

"Yes, I'm married, sure I am. I have a wife and three kids. My family consists of two boys and a girl."

Running between Strathgartner and Clyde River. Stopping and talking and sharing my story.
A young man demonstrating an artificial leg.
Speaking to the kids. Kindergarten classrooms and high school gyms. Talking about my life in BC. High school sports and family and friends. Talking of the day I learned about cancer. What it feels like to lose a leg. The grind of learning how to walk and then to run. Taking off my leg and showing them how it works. Making jokes about how I save lots of money on socks. Making it bigger to them than just a talk about cancer. It's a way of looking at life. Whether you have one leg or two you're going to come up against life. Every one of them can see themselves in me.

"Terry Fox has not yet acquired the knack of drumming up publicity for his cross- Canada Marathon of Hope run for cancer research. In some towns, the crowds are large and enthusiastic and in some towns, even if people have heard of Terry Fox, the fact that he is running through their town on a particular day remains unknown to them."

"Hear the fund-raising isn't going so well."
"It's not the problems with the running that's getting him down."

Enjoying the loneliness of the long-distance runner.
People offering to wash our clothes and clean the van.
Sending my leg off for another repair.

"It was pretty hard on Doug. It was almost as if there was two Terrys. The Terry who met with the crowds at night and charmed them in the gymnasiums, who seemed to want to reach out to everyone who was suffering and bring them some kind of relief. Then there was the Terry who was stern as iron the next day, who demanded that his drink be ready on time and his sock be dry and ready to put on whenever his good foot got too wet, and who did an all-day burn if Doug wasn't sure where the marker was along the roadside in the dark at five o'clock in the morning. And then when the run was over, Terry seemed to be able to switch to the hijinx on a dime, as if he was an entirely different person. Doug was finding it hard to roll with Terry's moods."

Potatoes growing in soil as red as can be.
White buildings with green trim.
Scallop-collecting on the beach at low tide.

When the sun comes up - right there on his face - a smooth groove - the camera moved in - toils for no reward - other people's pain - fought for the future - poison to me - malignant neoplasms - as far as relationships go.

What to do at the end of childhood? Soon I was going to need a job. How was I going to prepare myself for the rest of my life?

Seemed like a good idea to go to university. Spent a whole evening talking it over with Mom. As she talked about courses, I was thinking of nothing but sports.

Signed up for Kinesiology. Science of the body; the body as a servant of the mind. I'd have my sports and Mom would have her degree.

"You recall," the hare added,
"That last time, the tortoise won the race."

Running between Cornwall and Charlottetown. Shin splints, inflamed knee, broken toenails, bleeding, cysts.

An exhausted runner stopping to take a drink.

Forgetting about the five thousand miles. Forgetting about the marathons. Thinking one mile at a time. Doug stops the van and waits at every mile. From one telephone pole to the next. From one water-break to the next. Sometimes one stride is all I have in my head.

"While there can be no doubt of the personal appeal of Terry Fox to the crowds which greet him with such enthusiasm, there have undoubtedly been some disappointments for Terry, as there seems to be little consistency in the fundraising aspect of the Marathon of Hope."

Eating, phoning, sleeping.
Running, running, running.

A wise man teaching his son how to invest.
A cleaning lady sending in three hundred dollars.
Wanting to just go into the room and close the door.

"Terry's brother made all the difference. Darrell was champing at the bit to come out and join his brother, Terry, on the run, but their mom and dad insisted that Darrell finish his exams. Anyway, when they flew out and saw the bad blood between Terry and Doug – or maybe I should say the block of ice – they agreed that Darrell would be the perfect one to act as a buffer between the two. They never thought of replacing Doug. They realized how hard it was on Doug too – driving across Canada alone in the van and with Terry being as demanding as he is. It was a relief for Doug too – Doug and Darrell just shuffled the duties and things went a lot more smoothly after that. There was never any thought of firing Doug. There must have been times when Doug felt like quitting – he's only human after all – but he never did. He just went cold as ice – and Terry too."

Kids lining up outside a movie theatre.
A lady cutting a slice of fresh-baked bread.
Cars lining up to board a ferry.

"He's doing what very few people are able to do."
"He's lifting the spirits of a whole nation."

Hares lose, turtles win - me against myself - young man with tears in his eyes - move across the earth's surface - wounds which are being inflicted - had to do something - every drop of blood - choice of a story - a tree about to fall - to believe in miracles.

It was tough to sit through English classes. *Ode on an Urn* and *The Isles of Innisfree.* I was looking out the classroom window at the football team.

Wondering why I was in school. Wondering what to do with my life. I was the kind who always liked to have a plan.

Maybe I could be a high-school coach. Get to inspire a bunch of boys. The boys who think they don't have what it takes to play on the teams.

The pygmy didn't bow down to the giant.
Instead – he stood up high, on the tips of his toes.

A day in Charlottetown. Dizziness at times and double vision once in a while.

Kids laughing at a finger wiggling through a hole in a sock.

What people don't seem to understand is that I can't pay attention to my health. If I paid the kind of attention that the media and the doctors and my parents want me to pay I would probably quit. That's the one thing I just won't do. They're not even going to get me to stop and take a rest. A marathon a day, every day. That's the only way I'm going to make it through. The people who are most concerned are the people who are most in my way. The best are the kids at the schools. They never think about any problems with my legs. All they care about is that Terry runs every day.

"I make the numbers dance in a circle.
I make the numbers march in a line."

Filling the bucket with donations on a rural road.
Skipping another medical exam.
Tons of people lining the streets in Charlottetown.

"Equal rights and responsibilities, obligations and rewards.
Bound to each other with proverbial hoops of steel."

"The lightest materials constitute the continental crust; they remain at the surface and preserve some record of the long history of Earth's construction."

Seems that way
when things go wrong.

Ever want to just stay in bed?
Ever tempted to just say that's enough?
Ever tempted to shut it all down and fly back home?

A motel room in Borden-Carlton. Waiting to board the ferry for New Brunswick. Had another dizzy spell on the final run.

An athlete falling asleep in a soapy bathtub.

Feeling good about Prince Edward Island. Fundraising is going well but a lot of money is needed so it would be nice if everybody could help to pick up the pace. Nice to add another province to the list. Twenty-six miles a day, rain or shine. Some days a little less, some days a little more, but the average is always just about on the nose. Watched a hockey game last night. TV and newspaper coverage is good. Weather should soon be warming up. Told Doug not to mention the doctor. Don't ever mention my health! The artificial leg is taking a beating. It's not made for the kind of things I'm putting it through. What's left of the real leg is taking a beating too. Easing myself down into the bathtub. Nursing a battered and bruised stump night after night.

Chapter 4

Running across New Brunswick. Between Sackville and Memramcook. Hills of snow. Walls of wind. Troubles with the van.

A boy hugging his parents in a motel room.

I always break down on the phone. Every time I talk to my parents I start to cry. Nobody told me they would be coming. They could tell by the look on my face that I was surprised.

It's not a walk-hop. It's not a trot. It's running.

Riding in a fire truck around the town.
Running thirty miles in one day on the open road.
Hugging my parents as soon as I see them.

It's as close as I can get to running and it's harder than doing it on two legs.

"The materials that constitute the crust that now lies beneath the oceans are somewhat more dense."

It's the difference between running up a hill and running up a mountain.

So a young fellow sets out to run across Canada?
So what if cancer has cost him one of his legs?
What makes this front-page news or even page nine?

Running between Apohaqui and Norton. Artificial leg breaking down. Some towns don't know I'm coming through. Other towns break out the high school band.

A boy and a girl sitting at a table and writing a letter.

I don't let myself think of Rika. No thoughts about help with homework or writing the letter that asked for support. I don't let myself think of the doctors. No more x-rays until I get to the end of the run. I don't let myself think of the family. Mom and Dad and Fred and Judith. Darrell's right beside me, in the van and in the motels, so I have my family with me all the time. Don't cultivate your weaknesses; work on your strengths. That's what the coach always said and I live by that rule. If I thought about certain things they would drag me down. There'll be plenty of time for my future when I finish the run.

"Behind me, here in New Brunswick, the young Canadian runner, Terry Fox, is catching the imagination of people clear across Canada with his epic run. The sparse traffic, the lone runner and the slowly-moving van have become familiar images to the many Canadians who are following Terry's progress."

"Seems he's got the running down."
"How that boy can run like that is a wonder to me."

"Cancer is a group of diseases involving abnormal cell growth with the potential to invade or spread to other parts of the body. Not all tumours are cancerous; benign tumours do not spread to other parts of the body. Possible signs and symptoms include a lump, abnormal bleeding, prolonged cough, unexplained weight loss and a change in bowel movements. While these symptoms might indicate cancer, they might have other causes. Over one hundred cancers affect humans."

"The thing was, you couldn't get ahead of him. So competitive – you could tell that right away. He never wanted to let anyone get ahead. I used to run a lot when I was a teenager. Not so much lately but I'm still in pretty good shape. So I thought I'd jog along for a while and then stop and turn around and take a picture. For my mother – she was in a wheelchair and she'd been watching on TV. But I couldn't pull away. He gets in a groove with that running of his and he's always pretty focused. You got the feeling he could speed up any time. Probably ran a lot faster out in the country. Anyway, I let the photograph go. Gradually everyone fell away as we got to the edge of town. None of us had a way to get back so we all quit running and let him go. We let him run off into the distance on his own."

The long cool shade of a covered bridge.

A boy with potato chips and a bottle of pop.
Young deer romping like puppies in a meadow.

A series of barriers of pain - the people who know me - a prison without any hope - only thing I could think of - give all that you have - i or we - grind against the bones - dodging speeding cars - stretching himself too thin.

Life was good when I was eighteen. Spending time doing what I was good at. Gradually figuring out what I'd like to do with my life.

Living a life of routine. Home, school, track. Basketball, running, homework.

Getting ready for the rest of my life. A lot of decisions still to be made. Deciding to try to be the best person I could possibly be.

"Doors? Shutters?" the builder asked.
"I presume that they should also be extra-strong."

Running between Mecuctic and Northampton. I'm doing what I want to do. How many people can say that?

A runner who is grimacing in pain.

There's a pendulum inside me, and it swings very wide over to one side and back again. On the good days, everything is in harmony; on the bad days, all I seem to feel is the pain. People tell me I never smile when I run, so I guess the good days never show on my face.

"Terry Fox is an excellent speaker, and this crowd behind me has been energized by the speech that Terry has just given. His willingness to linger on and talk to people about the cause for which he is running is endearing him to hundreds of people along the route."

Searching for the marker from yesterday's run.
Going to bed at seven o'clock every evening.

Talking at three high schools in one day.
Eating almost all of a chocolate cake.
Phoning the Toronto Star once a week.

"I was surprised that he was such a passionate speaker. He was handsome and full of life and with masses of curly hair. Brimming with health from his daily runs with a deep tan and a muscular frame. He talked in simple terms. Told his story in a minimum of words. How he was living a normal life. Just another teenager growing up with family and friends in Port Coquitlam. Then an accident in his car. A minor fender-bender. And the next thing you know he was

living his life on one leg. Then he showed us his artificial leg. How it worked –
the springs and clamps and things. He said he always wore his shorts so people
could see. Said he wasn't ashamed of his stump. All the kids seemed amazed
that he was so open. So honest about his stump. We talked about it in class after
he left. He seemed to be living in a zone where the kids all hoped to be some
day – facing their problems, making adjustments and going on with their lives.
He didn't present himself as a victim – he was managing his life. They all felt he
was one of them. He made that day a very memorable day."

A truck loaded with vegetables headed for market.
A grandfather teaching his grandson how to fish.
Students waving from the windows of a bus.

"He's redefining what it is for us to be human."
"He makes us feel a whole lot better about ourselves."

Best investment advice - overcome big odds - talked in simple terms - the
mountain was there - rely on just myself - your feet have lotsa rock - gave those
kids my word - without its drawbacks - crying over the phone - peeling off my
bloody sock.

No more swearing when I lose. "Don't take it so much to heart, Terry.
You can't expect to be the winner in every game."
Trying hard to control my temper. Trying to lose with a bit more grace.
Mom kept telling me I should learn to lose with grace.
Deciding that winning was my life-long goal. You don't feel like swear-
ing when you win. No need for losing with grace when you're hoisting a trophy
and grinning from ear to ear.

The man returned to the oracle.
"Please repeat your words of yesterday," he asked.

Running between Maliseet and Tobique Narrows. It's courage and not
foolishness. I'll keep going until I die.
A group of rowdy teenagers in a restaurant.
Resting at the end of the days. Reading the mail or glancing at the news
or just sitting in the van door to get some fresh air. Joking around with the guys.
– Spraying water on each other. – Smearing catsup on a shirt. – Grabbing my
artificial leg. – Giving a demonstration. – Holding it upside down like a cane.
– This is how you do it! – This is how you walk with an artificial leg! Kidding
around with the guys but feeling low. If I keep them up, they'll keep me up, and
I need the energy to keep pushing past the pain.

"The continual release of radiogenic heat from the Earth's interior takes place along the sea-floor in the middle of oceans, and it is this process that causes continental tectonic plates to move across the Earth's surface at rates of approximately three to fifteen centimetres per year."

How is the money going to be spent?
Pheasant dinners and limousines for those in charge?
Will every penny be spent like you would spend it yourself?

"Rocky crags within sight of the sea. Deep valleys with brambles and thorns. A brutal sun beating down on Phidippides's head. Not a drop of water to drink. Grit in his teeth; gleam in his eye. Phidippides pounded along the trail for mile after mile."

Ship Harbour - Lake Charlotte - Jeddore Oyster Ponds - Head of Jeddore - Smith Settlement - Musquodoboit Harbour - Gaetz Brook - Head of Chezzsetcook - Porters Lake - East Preston - Loon Lake - Dartmouth - Halifax - Bedford - Lower Sackville - Windsor Junction - Fall River - Enfield - Elmsdale - Lantz - Milford Station - Shubenacadie - Stewiake - Fort Ellis - Brentwood - Brookfield - Hilden - Truro - Londonderry Station - Lornevale.

"The fourteen days that Terry Fox has spent running in New Brunswick have yielded four hundred and six more miles for the run across Canada, the total having now reached one thousand four hundred and fifty-two miles."

"I have a house not far from my parents. Live there with my wife. Soon our kids will be of age to head off to school."

Running between Argosy and Grand Falls. This run is not a waste. I want to set an example that will never be forgotten.
A family sitting down to a full-course meal.
I'm glad I had supper with Mom and Dad. A feast of Atlantic seafood. Doug was sitting beside me. Mom and Dad were across the table. Everyone else was all around. Everybody was chatting away and having a good time. I was starting to feel like a phony. My leg was really sore and it was making me bitchy. I was taking things out on Doug and he was taking things out on me. My parents were there to try to heal the wound. They knew there was something wrong when I started to cry on the phone. Then we fought in front of my parents. I lit into Doug and he lit into me. Doug is sick and tired of the van. – I'm sick and tired of Doug. We probably looked like friends to the firemen, but we didn't get anything settled. I begged them to send me Darrell. My parents said they'd see what they could do.

"People are waiting hours to greet Terry Fox as he runs through the province and many have travelled miles to donate to the cause of cancer research in his name. The enthusiasm of this young runner, as he makes his way across Canada, is becoming an inspiration to more and more people as his name and purpose gradually become better known."

"It's beautiful just to watch him moving along."
"He's overcome a lot just to get this far."

Cars honking as I run along the main street.
A boy asking his grandfather about water and rock.
Waiting for the thunder and lightning to stop.

"A reporter asked Terry about the loneliness of the long-distance runner and he said he never felt such a thing. He said he'd always enjoyed running, even when he had two legs. And he spent over a year running alone – getting ready for the Marathon of Hope – when he was back in BC. He said he just runs along and thinks about things – how many miles he's covered – how many miles are still left – how the fund-raising is going – how cancer will someday be cured – what he'd like to say that night at the next reception. He said he always looked forward to meetings with the kids most of all. And late in every run he said he would think about a hot shower and his favourite food."

A group of girls whirling around in a Scottish reel.
A vegetable stand along the roadside.
An old dog panting hello at the side of a road.

Concentrate your focus - little time to lose - major plate collisions - something you have to pay for - looking through your own eyes - two hops and a stride - strengthened by crippling blows - always have, always will - undermining the cause - kids in the cancer wards.

Family. Sports on TV. Taking Rika out to the movies or to a dance.
Grinding away at the books. Seemed to be a lot of Math in Kinesiology. Whoever would have thought that the body was so complex?
Now and then a good word from the coach. One day he read out the list. Great feeling to know I'd made the varsity team.

"I am sure," the tortoise added,
"That this time the hare will run a different race."

Running between Sainte-Anne-de-Madawasska and Grande Isle. You're only down if you think you're down. And I'm not down.

A man slapping a drink from another one's hand.

It was difficult smiling and chatting with all those people. Nicest people in the world. How could they know that Doug and I were at each other's throats? But it wasn't so easy as just getting along. Doug was poison to me if he didn't believe in what I was doing. Let him try running every mile across a whole country. Let me sit in the van and laze along. Maybe that would shake him up. The food was delicious, the people were nice, but I couldn't just sit there and fill my face and smile at everybody and act like a phony. When I'm unhappy I let people know. That's why I take it all out on Doug. I just had to tell my parents what was going on.

"While Terry Fox, reportedly, was a young man who was not used to public speaking, he has blossomed into a truly inspirational speaker, one who is willing to take time to talk to groups along the route of his Marathon of Hope run. He is especially good at establishing a rapport with students, and is visiting as many classrooms as his running schedule permits."

Getting as close as I can get to a two-legged run.
Daydreaming about my run through Stanley Park.

A person talking about a safety-harness.
People giving their hard-earned cash.
Birds singing at sunrise every morning.

"Terry was stubborn as a mule. The one thing he wouldn't let us talk about was the run. Anything else was fine, but not the run. Or his health – that was a topic we didn't touch. A grim machine while he was running – a goofy kid when he was done. That's why all the high-jinks. He made us a lot more goofy than we wanted to be. I wasn't the kind to kid around but I got the idea early that it was what he needed. That was why there was so much tension in the early days. He didn't have an outlet for all that steam. That's why we acted like kids in the restaurants. We tried to show respect to the waitresses – no food on the tables or the chairs – but anything else was fair game. Splotches of catsup on someone's hair – a stream of mustard down someone's back – pull out someone's pants and drop some butter inside. It was exactly what Terry needed. It made us all equal – just a bunch of goofy kids. But it was only when the miles were finished. There was nothing more dead-serious than the run."

A lobster trap tied to the roof of a car.
Logging trucks chugging up a hill.
A boy bouncing a ball against a wall.

"He's uniting us into one positive force for good."

"He's rolling back the darkness day by day."

What kind of story - my victory over you - going through a nightmare - a messenger would arrive - the law was the law - as swift as the tortoise - the qualities that you will draw on - given up smiling - a serious disease - the very image.

It comes at you out of the blue. You don't even think about cancer as you go from day to day. Basketball and schoolwork and family and good times with the guys.

I was driving my beat-up old car – Cortina, 1968, green. Lost my concentration and crunched right into the back of a half-ton truck. Totalled the car, but I got off with what I thought was just a scratch.

Banged my knee on the dashboard. Some lingering pain after practices and games. Went to the doctor, finally, to get a minor thing put right.

I feel equal to the giant, thought the pygmy.
My strengths against his strengths, any day.

Running between Moulin-Mourneaut and Digelis. Can't let myself daydream about having two legs.
An athlete rubbing lineament into his thigh.
Sometimes the body turns against itself. At first it's a pain in your knee. Then you find you can barely walk. Then you go to see a doctor. He says it's osteogenic sarcoma. A malignant inner-disease. It breaks down bone and muscles and tendons. There's no reversing it once it starts. It moves through the bloodstream all over the body. It's either immediate surgery or certain death.

"I make the numbers bow down before me.
I make the numbers sing me a song."

Fighting off the pain one day at a time.
Greg Scott running beside me for about six miles.
Crawling into the van to cry and sleep.

"Every clause has been written carefully.
There is nothing you need to fear."

"The Canadian Shield, which occupies the centre of the country, is so named because its outline suggests the shape of the shields which were carried by soldiers in the days of hand-to-hand combat."

The world in just one person;

Just one person in the world.

A dollar from every Canadian for a cure for cancer?
Aren't there fifty diseases or maybe a hundred or more?
How many dollars would it take to relieve all the pain?

A church parking lot between Saint-Antenin and Riviere-de-Loup. Soon be out of New Brunswick and into Quebec. Waiting for cheeseburgs and chips. Sent the guys out to get some. Maybe if I lie here and think about food I can fall asleep.

A young man looking at pictures on the walls of a bedroom.

I've had three thousand people on the main street of a little village cheering every word and putting their money into pails, and I've had a town of ten thousand people sitting home and watching TV while their mayor and a couple of councillors give me a cheque for a hundred dollars. Some people invite me in to supper and have a shower and stay overnight. Some put me up in the beds of their sons and daughters away at school. Then in other places they stare from the sidewalk, wondering at this kid on one leg who's running through the middle of their town. But I can't let that be the run. It has to be something that takes in all of this and just keeps going on and on. It can't be something that goes or stops on whether people know who I am and why I'm here. I can't let it set me up or drag me down.

Chapter 5

Running in Quebec. My fifth province out of ten. Running along beside the St. Lawrence River.

A man tossing a ball to children across a fence.

Can't believe the power of the water. Can't believe the power of the wind. Feel a tremendous sense of a barrier. People here should know more English – I should know more French. Phoning up a local newspaper and having someone answer in French is just a dead-end. I can't give them an interview and they can't ask me questions. But cancer is always cancer. It knows everybody's name. Anybody in the world could lose a leg. Gotta figure how to communicate. The towns in Quebec are very beautiful. Every village has a church with a glistening steeple. Kids are playing outside at recess but I can't tell them about my leg. Should be better in Quebec City and Montreal.

How many people do something they really believe in?

A lady in her nightgown offering coffee.
Dodging speeding cars on narrow roads.
A story-teller asking whether it's I or we.

I just wish people would realize that anything's possible if you try.

"Rocks of the Shield underlie the interior of the continent beneath the Rocky Mountains, as well as the interior plains of Canada and the United States, where the sedimentary rocks of the Interior Platform cover them."

Dreams are only made if people try.

Is this a success or is this a failure?
All that running and how much cash?
What is the point if not enough people care to give?

Running, running, running. Between Monmagny and Berthier-sur-mer. Farmers and logging trucks and not much else.

A policeman talking to a boy at the side of a road.

People forcing me off the road. Honking their horns and roaring by, doing eighty miles an hour. The road seems very narrow. It seems to shrink before my eyes. Tried running on the four-lane highway. No towns, no crowds, no fundraising. But at least there was room to run. After two days, the police said I have to take the side-roads. – Too dangerous! – Can't let you run! So I'm running along the secondary roads.

"Young Terry Fox looks over his shoulder as the massive lumber trucks and high-speed cars whiz by him on this lonely stretch of the Trans-Canada highway. As he moves so deliberately along this busy roadway, just inside the border of the province of Quebec, Terry is entering the fifth stage of his Marathon of Hope cross-Canadian run for cancer research."

"Must be lonely out on that road when you're all alone."

"Must be tough when you come to a town and there's no one to welcome you."

"Cancer refers to any one of a large number of diseases which are characterized by the development of abnormal cells which divide uncontrollably and have the ability to infiltrate and destroy normal body tissue. Cancer often has the ability to spread throughout your body. Cancer is the second-leading cause of death in our society, but survival rates are improving for many types of cancer, thanks to improvements in cancer-screening and cancer-treatment."

"There was that kid again. Always running at the side of the road. I saw him in Nova Scotia and again in New Brunswick. I rolled down the window so I could get a better look. How the hell could he keep it up on just one leg? I wondered if he'd see me if I waved. Geeze – he did! He waved a little wave. Gave me a look. I wondered if I should stop. Turn the car around and go back. Stop the car and get out and talk. But I didn't think that was what he wanted. I couldn't sleep that time in New Brunswick. I knew I was going to be haunted by this guy for quite a while. Just to think what it must take to do what he was doing. A kid with one leg who was running all over the map."

A raging river emptying the water from half a continent.
Fiddle music drifting into the night.
White sails on the river below a town.

A boy who listens to children - hold the persians off - name and purpose
- nature of the value - another person's eyes - at the highest possible level - how
many terry foxes - concentrate your focus - banging into a half-ton truck - what
to compare it with.

Blood tests, bone scans, x-rays. In a ward with eight little boys. Why would there be all this fuss for a pain in the knee?

Sad looks on the faces of my parents as they came to see me one day. In my family, you don't keep secrets. "We'll give it to you straight, Terry – the doctor says its cancer of the bone."

"It's cancer, all right, Terry," the doctor told me. "That's what every test has shown. I'm afraid you're going to have to lose the leg."

"Oh, extra-extra strong," the man said to the builder.
"And nail them shut as soon as I get my family inside."

Running between Saint-Apolonaire and Sainte-Flavien. Nice weather but there haven't been any crowds.

A runner throwing himself into a ditch to avoid a car.

Running on the pavement. When I hear a car I jump on the grass. People blare the horn and shout. There hasn't been any publicity. – Not an article. – Not an interview. One guy stopped his truck and insisted on giving me a ride. I kept pointing at the camper-van. – I've got a ride! – I'm running for cancer! Couldn't make him understand. No ride! – No ride! – No ride! Cancer! – Cancer! – Cancer! Didn't seem to understand. Didn't offer any money. He finally got into his truck and drove away. At the next town, there were twenty people waiting.

"The question of Terry Fox's stamina, as he endures a gruelling marathon-a-day pace across this nation seems to have been answered, so far, in Terry's favour. Though weather, road conditions and temporary illness have all been factors on a daily basis, the intrepid young runner has managed to average twenty six miles a day for the entire length of the run so far."

Searching for the marker from yesterday's run.
Getting as close as I can get to a two-legged run.

Playing Hank Snow songs in the van.
Big trucks roaring by on a two-lane highway.
A man offering to phone his friends for donations.

"The problem wasn't with the prosthesis. Oh, I could make a few adjustments, but that was never the point. The problem was with the boy. He wouldn't allow the bleeding stump to heal. They told me he would be stubborn. They said he wouldn't listen. Sure enough, he came at me like a bull. I said that the prosthesis is doing its job. I could adjust the springs a bit but it wasn't designed for a marathon a day. I swear his eyes got red. Like a bull when you flash a cape. 'I don't have time to rest! I don't have time to heal! I don't have time to see a doctor! So just adjust the springs and leave me be! I don't want any advice! If I listened to the doctors I'd still be lounging around on my bed in Port Coquitlam!' His face was flushed and his eyes were red. So I kept my advice to myself. I told him I'd do the best I could with the springs."

A lady and her granddaughter mixing paint.
A tall white steeple pointing high above the village.
A girls' baseball team warming up.

"There is a glow that such people emanate."
"There are people who themselves are sources of light."

Ruin the whole campaign - a partnership of equals - making it bigger to them - for us to be human - wondering who I am- to give all that I have - not enough me - pick the one you want - bending over in terrible pain - I will grant release.

Talks with the doctors. Pamphlets to read. Hard to believe that "the cancer patient" was going to be me.

In a cancer ward with the kids. No age-limit on cancer. Some kids know cancer before they know how to ride a trike.

Then the day finally came. In with two legs, out with one. The second half of my life had just begun.

"You cannot draw yesterday's water from the well," said the oracle.
"Today's pronouncement is that of yesterday in reverse."

Running between Daveluyville and Saint-Cyrille-de-Wendover. Pretty quiet on the highway. Once in a while, a small crowd gathers and wishes me luck.

Drops of blood in the bowl of an artificial leg.

The artificial leg is holding up. I've asked it to do a lot. More than any other amputee has asked it to do. Actually it's taken quite a beating over the miles. I've had something fixed in almost every province. Always something that can't take the pace. Maybe a valve or a spring or a gear. You take the old one out and put a new one in. The secret to being a runner is to make yourself into a machine. A machine that renews itself. When anything breaks down you search around for something to replace it. All the replacements and repairs have to come from inside.

"The Shield is composed of ancient rocks, including some that are among the oldest rocks on Earth, possibly more than four billion years old."

Why not turn your back on cancer?
Weren't you told you were cancer-free?
Aren't you letting cancer dominate your life?

"Phidippides reached the top of a hill. Dry as dust; the sun beating down. Covered in sweat; pausing for breath. Just a moment to look ahead to see where he was. Sparta! He could see it in the distance! Won't take long to deliver the message. Athens and Sparta; both of them Greek. He breathed a sigh of relief. The return won't seem as daunting. The message will be that help is on the way."

Londonderry - Thompson Station - Oxford - Springhill - Amherst - Ft. Lawrence - Aulac - Watley - Pont de Bute - Jolicure - Baie Verte - Port Elgin - Timber River - Bayfield - Borden-Carlton -Tryon - Crapaud - Victoria - South Melville - Bonshaw - Strathgartner - Clyde River - Cornwall - Charlottetown - Sackville - Memramcook - Moncton - Mapleton - Lutes Mountain - Berry Mills - Steves Mountain - Petitcodiac - Annagance - Penobsquis.

"While here in Quebec, Terry Fox has run three hundred and ninety-eight miles across the province and has raised his Marathon of Hope total to one thousand eight hundred and fifty miles."

"Later today, we'll all get in the car and go for a drive. We'll go to my parents' house. My brothers and sister and their families will all be there and we'll all have a big barbecue in the back yard."

Running between Sainte Madeleine and Boucheville. Skies clear and highways bare. Traffic slow on these secondary roads.
A shy person hanging his head to a burst of applause.
I'm glad I gave that speech at Dartmouth Vocational School. That little speech about Doug. – How hard it must be to sit there in the van day after day. – Getting me water every mile and a dry sock whenever I need it. – Putting up with me when I get irritable and tired. I take out my frustrations on him and I know it's wrong. I'm the one that gets all the praise and Doug just stands there during the receptions and hears everybody praising Terry Fox. So I told the kids I wanted to talk about Doug. – How Doug has the courage to put up with me. –

To understand how tired I get and how irritable I get when I get frustrated. I led everyone in a round of applause for Doug. I did it for Doug but mostly I did it for myself. I couldn't fight Doug in the van and in the motel rooms and then go out and smile and wave and have everybody saying that Terry Fox is a wonderful guy. I couldn't face people if I was living a phony life.

"Publicity has been a major difficulty here in Quebec, as the handicapped young marathon runner, Terry Fox, speaks no French. It makes it almost impossible to give interviews to the local newspapers and television stations or to give his inspirational speeches to the crowds along the way."

"Hear the Ontario Cancer Society's taking him on."
"They'll make him a household name if anyone can."

Watching the Stanley Cup playoffs.
Phoning ahead to ask for an interview.
Using a bullhorn to wake up all the sleepers in town.

"We had trouble in Quebec. The languages were the problem. None of us spoke French. A little bit of high school French and that was all. It was fine in the big cities – Quebec and Montreal – but you get a little ways out of town and they all speak French. We went to a restaurant one time. Small town along the highway. We all managed to order a sandwich and some soup. Then Terry figures it out. The word for washroom. So he says 'Sale de baigne?' and the waitress doesn't have a clue. 'Non.' No sale de baigne. So Terry says 'Washroom?' So the waitress says 'Mushroom?' and we all laugh. So we stuck to the chemical toilet for most of Quebec. The van stunk but what were we supposed to do? Turns out the word is 'toilette'. Got to Ontario before we were told. 'Toilet' equals 'toilette'. Turns out French and English aren't as far apart as they seem."

An old fellow carving wood outside a store.
A cottage with a boat tied up at a dock.
A crowd strolling along on market day.

The basic core of life - come up against life - run a different race - the nightmare-run - how tired and how alone - never lost himself - narrow pathway, steep climb - training my sights - tumbling through his mind - grant as a boon.

Chemotherapy, loss of hair, missing leg. Funny cards that wished me well. Asking myself if I was ready to lie down and die.

What to do? What to do? I cried a few tears – a lot of tears in fact – while I was wondering what I could do on only one leg.

Then a boy who was whispering his dreams was cut short by the call for lights-out. I woke up to a midnight kerfuffle as the attendants whispered and worked. Next morning the bed was all made and there was no one there.

"For tomorrow," sighed the god of the forest,
"The hare will be a tortoise and the tortoise will be a hare,
But I wish they wouldn't pester me with prayer."

Montreal. City Hall. Plenty of attention to the run at last. Reporters. TV cameras. Nice to see.

A one-legged runner rubbing his ankle at a picnic table.

Meeting the mayor of Montreal. Glad he could find the time. Seems to be quite friendly. Took his secretary a while to answer our call. Everybody at City Hall seems to speak English. Makes it easier to talk. The photographers are from the daily papers. Some reporters as well. A few questions and then they fade away. There are two kinds of mayors in my opinion. Those who are serving in office and those who are running for office. They look about the same in the photographs though the ones who are running for office have bigger grins. The ones who are serving in office are just doing their jobs. They're the ones who stay behind after the photographers have left and have a talk. The kind who mention their wives and children. They have relatives who've died. The ones who are running for office don't have the time. Well, time to get back to the run. Nice, though, to get some publicity in Montreal.

"Perhaps the biggest question to ask, as the Terry Fox Marathon of Hope nears the Ontario border, is as to whether the effort which Terry is expending, in his gruelling run across the vast surface of the Canadian landscape, is drawing the donations that Terry Fox expected to raise when he began this epic enterprise."

Coming to a city with nothing organized for us.
Running on a slanted roadway on a painful ankle.

Having a t-shirt made up in French as I run through Quebec.
Ignoring everything that would interfere with the run.
Making adjustments to the prosthesis.

"I was sitting on the hotel stairs. They had the door closed to the room. They didn't seem all that positive when they asked me to leave. Did the best presentation I could. Told them everything I knew. I told them 'This could be what we need'. I didn't want to say things like 'Godsend' or 'gold mine' or things like that. They were all hard-headed people. Wouldn't be swept away by a speech. 'Do we support this kid or not?' 'Do we send our man to work with him when he gets to Ontario?' 'Is he legitimate or just a fluke?' 'Just wait outside awhile and we'll take a vote.' I had my suitcase packed in my room. I was hoping they'd give him a chance. He was the best thing to happen to cancer since I'd been around. Of course, I didn't say that in my speech. Something like that would only get me a room full of frowns. Then I heard a noise and somebody opened the door."

A chateau perched high above the river.
A school bus inching along a dusty road.
A flock of nuns waiting to cross a cobbled street.

"He's the grandson, the son and the brother of every Canadian."
"Every one of us is taking him to our hearts."

Finding the things inside - looked cancer in the face - a way of looking at life - positive force for good - one more soldier - a movie of a run - provide the highest yields - undreamed-of proportions - a bag of balloons - didn't know what to do.

Life in the cancer ward; death in the cancer ward. The two of them side-by-side in every bed. All anyone wanted to do was to have a good life.

Lying awake in the cancer ward. Listening to the screams. The screams got more and louder as the night went on.

Who was going to ease this pain? There had to be something that some-one could do to help these kids. I kept telling myself that somewhere the hurting must stop.

The giant turned around and noticed the pygmy.
It's not the size; it's the stature, thought the giant.
If only I could see inside his mind.

Taking a tour of Montreal. A beautiful city. Nice to look around.
A handsome young man buying a hotdog from a street-vendor.
Listening to the guide, of course, but thinking about the run. Delaying the run so we get to Ottawa on Canada Day. First day without running since I started in St. John's. Don't sleep well if I'm not exhausted. Try to drive myself to exhaustion every day. Better to sleep than to lie awake and think. – How's the fundraising going? – How many miles still to go? – How's the stump holding up? – Springs okay in your artificial leg? I toss and turn and try to sleep. Lots of questions without any answers. But the biggest one of all is the one I know the answer to. – Are the kids still crying in the cancer wards at night?

"That's all very well," said the tightrope-walker.
"But what do you do when all of the numbers break out of their cage?"

People stopping their cars and offering a lift.
Shaking the dizziness out of my head.
A warm reception on Sherbrooke Street in Montreal.

"Just sign the contract – first things first.
Any adjustments can be improvised as we go."

"The construction of the Shield involved the collision and build-up of a large number of tectonic plates, beginning more than three billion years ago, and was largely completed by about 800 million years ago."

As bad as things can get.
Why go on?

Why not spend your life in the rec-room?
Watching hockey games on TV?
Collecting your disability payments and drifting through life?

Flopping on the bed. TV flickering in the dark. Asked to hold up the run for a while in Montreal.
A television flickering on a figure on a bed.
It's the body against the body. It's the mind against the mind. It's like the movies where the alien thing is inside you. You're being taken over by a force from another dimension. You're still free in your mind but the dark force is gaining ground. Taking over all the patients in the beds of the cancer wards. Everybody around you being attacked by something that's eating them alive and you're lying awake in the dark and hearing their screams. And you're thinking – thinking – thinking. – It's gradually taking over my body. – It's gradually eating away at everything I know of as me. – What is there that can stop it? – How is this nightmare going to end? – Am I going to die in the night and disappear?

Chapter 6

Hawkesbury, at the bridge. Crossing the Ottawa River into Ontario. The high school band thumping away. Balloons released and drifting up over the trees.

Two boys collecting money from a crowd.

The local community centre. Shaking everybody's hand. Three cheers from a pretty-big crowd. The announcer calls it a walk and then calls it a run. It's the first thing I always correct, but I don't need to now. People have driven here from all over. Wanting to donate and shake my hand. A feeling that things are going to be just great from now on.

This isn't soul-searching.

Shoppers clapping in the Sparks Street Mall.
A sign with miles-to-date and miles-to-go.
Run, eat, sleep. Run, eat, sleep.

I'm not trying to find something.

"The core of most of the world's major continents was created by the same plate-tectonic process."

I've found what I want.

What is the value of a hockey player?
What is the value of a baseball star?

Why would you want to hear a whole stadium chanting your name?

Running between L'Original and Alfred. The Cancer Society of Ontario is going full-out.

Snowflakes drifting down on an empty street.

Thanking Bill for what he did. It was Bill who convinced them that they should take me on. What a difference it's going to be. It's going to be better here in Ontario. You can be running down a road – flakes of snow and biting wind – and no one knows it. You know the next town is going to have an empty main street. Then you run down the same kind of road and everyone sees you on national TV and there's a thousand people waiting on the sidewalk when you run through their town. It makes the run a whole lot easier. Still the dizziness and the blood on the shorts and the breakdowns with the springs in the leg, but it sure makes all of the pain seem a lot more worth-while.

"The sunrise catches Terry Fox, who is running behind me here, as he makes his way into the Province of Ontario. The Terry Fox run for cancer is promising to become a phenomenon in Ontario, as he explodes onto the scene in a burst of media attention which is like nothing that has been seen in the enter-tainment industry."

"Overnight he's the biggest star in all of Canada."
"Everything he does is automatically front-page news."

"Cancer is caused by changes, called mutations, to the DNA within cells. The DNA inside a cell is packaged into a large number of individual genes, each of which contains a set of instructions telling the cell what functions to perform, as well as how to grow and divide. Errors in the instructions can cause the cell to stop its normal function and might allow a cell to become cancerous. A gene mutation can instruct a healthy cell to allow rapid growth, fail to stop uncontrolled cell-growth, and make mistakes when repairing DNA errors. These mutations are the most common ones which are found in cancer, but many other gene mutations can contribute to its cause."

"Our teacher introduced Terry and he stood at the front of the class and he talked about the cancer and how he'd lost his leg. Then it got even more in-teresting. He took off the leg and showed us how it worked. It has a valve and springs and a bucket and straps and things. Then we all went outside and started to run with him. Our teacher had told us so we all had our gym clothes on. But no one said anything about how we were going to get back to the school. And he was moving pretty fast. He stayed out in front of the kids and I was getting pretty tired. I was getting really worried. We were all running along with Terry but I was starting to worry that we were getting too far from the school. Our teacher runs all the time so she was okay. Finally, our teacher stopped. Terry kept going and didn't look back. We all caught our breath. I couldn't talk but one of the kids said 'I think he's gonna make it.' Then we all set out for the long walk back to the school."

A tractor ploughing furrows in a field.
Groups of shoppers moving slowly through a mall.
The tallest free-standing structure in the world.

Eaten by a shark - see themselves in me - a grim machine - every blade of grass - two steep traps - the sun on my face - the culminating events - just like in a movie - spirit will never die - the dark side.

At first, I didn't know whether I was going to live or die. I saw healthy bodies turning into skeletons; I saw smiles turning into grimaces of pain. When I turned out to be one of the lucky ones, I figured it was only right to give something back.

The cancer ward is a place that haunts your thoughts forever. It stays inside you and you can't just walk away. You've seen something that has bored right into your brain.

I'm not a great reader of pamphlets. I just skim them and toss them aside. But I could tell that more dollars were needed to ease the pain.

"Come to the window, little fellow," the father said to his son.
"Such a sight I no longer hoped to see."

Ottawa is beautiful. Enjoying the Sparks Street Mall. Cafés and shops and restaurants. Stopping and chatting and saying hello. Shoppers enjoying the sunshine. Having a cool drink in the shade.

Holiday crowds posing for pictures with a curly-haired boy.

Slowing the pace right down to a walk. What a beautiful sunny day. Hundreds of people out for the sunshine and a stroll. The crowds have been good since Hawkesbury. Everybody seems to know. The problem has always been to get out the word. Trying to tell them about the reason. Not enough to just wave at the crowds. Hope the media keeps telling the story. Don't want it to be a celebrity game. It's nice that people want to see me. Hope they also want to give. Nice to have such a group of runners. Want to show them how I can move. Soon be out on the streets and running. Nice to stroll along the mall but nicer to run.

"The media has a new darling, in Terry Fox, the young runner whose determination to run a marathon a day on only one leg in order to raise funds for cancer victims has caught the imagination of an enchanted public clear across Canada."

Telling people that cancer knows everybody's name.
Telling a reporter that I am not in search of myself.

Someone telling me that I should smile more as I run.
A person who is investing in what he loves.
Sharing a lobster dinner with a bunch of firemen.

"His speech was really moving. Really heart-felt. It was just a small crowd. You got the feeling he only stopped for a moment to say hello and catch his breath. Only ten of us or so on that stretch of highway. Sweat was pouring down his forehead and on his cheeks. The steam was coming off his shoulders as he was talking. He told us about the run and about cancer and how the money was going to be used to help the kids. I had a cooler so I gave him a can of pop. As he was drinking I told him how much I admired him. Not everyone was willing to do what he was doing. Then I took off my Canada pin and offered it to him. He asked me to pin it on his shirt and I did. Later, I saw him running through the city on TV. He was giving a talk to what must have been a thousand people over a microphone and the camera moved in and there was my Canada pin."

Two ladies patiently working on a quilt.
Fir trees growing out of rock.
A painter setting up an easel.

"He can be proud of himself for what he is accomplishing."
"He is one of those who makes everyone feel proud."

Singing at the top of their voices - I know who I am - remains unknown
- a minor thing put right - never lost himself - early days left scars - as if he was
my son - crawling into the van - a person going for a jog - give all that you have.

It was the screams in the cancer ward that did it. How could I lie there at night and let those screams go on? I decided that I had to do something to relieve the pain.

So I decided to run across Canada. It was the only thing I could think of to try to raise funds. Ask every Canadian to give one dollar to stop the screams.

I'd read a magazine article about an amputee who'd run in the New York Marathon. How much money could I raise for cancer research if I asked people to sponsor me if I was to run a marathon every day? How many miles would that be, I wondered, as I tried to drown out the screams.

On Monday the mountain was there.

Slate grey, snowy peak.
It looked as if the mountain would never move.

A media scrum on Parliament Hill. Flashbulbs flashing and reporters scribbling as we talk.

Two men surrounded by reporters and television cameras.

The Prime Minister is wondering who I am. They told us he just got back from a trip over-seas. Catching him in the hall after Question Period. Looks great in his spiffy suit. Carnation in his button-hole. Don't think he's dressed to run a few miles with me. The aide who is with him seems surprised. We were told to go to his office over the phone. Someone sent us here to the hall when we got inside. He asks me what I'm running for. – I tell him I'm running for cancer. I ask him to come out and run with me. – He tells me he doesn't have time. The cameras take it all in. The reporters listen and write. Me in my sweat-stained shorts. – Him in his natty suit. I show him my artificial leg. – We smile as we shake hands. It doesn't matter that he doesn't know me. Tonight it'll be all across Canada on the evening news.

"One of the last major plate collisions which was involved in the assembly of the Canadian Shield is named the Grenville Orogeny."

What do people want from a celebrity?
What do celebrities want from their fans?
What is the nature of the value that is being exchanged?

"Phidippides was running. The sun was blazing down, but for Phidippides it was what he thought of as a nightmare-run. He was running back to his general. He'd been to Sparta and given the message, but he had nothing to show to his fellows for all his pain. A leisurely conference; the gods would be angry; why should Sparta send lambs to the slaughter for Athens' gain? The aches in the joints; the sickening message; the torturing sun. Still he kept to a brutal pace. One foot up and one foot down. The Persians were massing for the attack. There were very few Athenians. At least he'd be one more soldier to make the stand."

McCully - Sussex East - Sussex - Lower Cove - Apohaqui - Norton - Bloomfield - Passakeag - Hampton - French Village - Quispamis - Rothsay - Saint John - Acamac - Grand Bay-Westfield - Welsford - Geary - Camp Gagetown - Oromocto - Fredericton - Mazerelle Settlement - Prince William - Pokiok - Southampton - Meductic - Northampton - Flemington - Woodstock - Waterville - Florenceville-Bristol - Knoxford - Muniac - Perth-Andover - Maliseet - Tobique Narrows - Four Falls - Argosy - Grand Falls.

"As he approaches Ottawa, Terry Fox is also closing in on the one thousand nine hundred and forty-one mile mark in his epic journey across the vast expanse of Canada."

"And I also run in marathons. Yes, even at my age. I guess you remember how I always liked to run."

Landsdowne Park. Sunny day, white clouds, blue sky. What a perfect day for a football game.
A one-legged boy kicking a football to a roar of applause.
Standing under the stands at the football stadium. Ottawa versus Saskatchewan. Watched it on TV but never thought about what it would be like to run on the field. Nervous, nervous, nervous. It's been a great reception in Ontario – bigger crowds at every stop – but nervous about the reception I'm going to get. Getting the signal and running onto the field. Overwhelmed by the roar of the crowd. Sixteen thousand people. Tony Gabriel holding the ball. Wish I'd been able to practice. Which foot am I going to use? Not bad. Got away a good one. Can't believe the standing ovation. Loudest roar I've ever heard. The announcer talking of cancer. Hope they hear him over the cheers. Glad I didn't stumble. Surprised to be given the ball. Surprised to see tears in his eyes. Sixteen thousand cheering people. Holding the football up and waving. Don't forget about cancer research! The cheering goes on and on. Making my way to a seat to watch the game.

"Terry Fox has been kept busy here in Ontario. He has met the Prime Minister and the Governor General, thrown out the football in front of thousands of cheering fans, run through towns with thousands of well-wishers lining the sidewalks, and is attending as many fund-raisers and rallies as he possibly can."

"He even got a mention on American TV."
"Don't know how he stuck with it when nobody knew his name."

Rolling over and trying to sleep.
An ancient tree about to fall in a forest.
Darrell dodging among the cars with a donation can.

"I don't know how Terry did it. He had a mind like two steel traps. He could talk to the Prime Minister or the Governor General of Canada and come across as what he was – a serious young man on an important mission. And I'd be standing there in my shorts. And Terry of course would be in his. He always insisted that we never dress up on occasions like that. And he'd be drilling these important people. Telling them how urgent this was. How cancer can be beaten if they'd just do their jobs and spread the word. And I'd be thinking of the other Terry – the one who'd rub a stinking sock in my face – the one who'd whoop and snap a wet towel an inch from my arse. And he never got the two mixed up. For me it was a matter of trying to keep a straight face. I don't think Terry had that trouble. He never lost himself for a moment. Straight face and serious talk – a goofy grin and a wet towel. The secret was that both were Terry Fox."

People scattering to avoid a thundershower.
Horses grazing quietly in a field.
A waterfall that drains five great lakes.

Discovering things about yourself - two terrys - every word you say - a place to rest - a man who seeks no reward - human after all - paying the highest price - playing hank snow songs - to relieve all the pain - influence over me.

I'd never gotten to see the rest of Canada. I thought I'd see Canada the way very few people ever do. Someone in the cancer ward said, "See Canada and die."

One thousand, seven hundred and ninety footsteps in a mile. One hundred thousand and seven hundred and ninety footsteps in a hundred miles. Maybe that was wrong – maybe it was more – maybe I should have paid more attention in high school Math.

I let the miles take care of themselves. The first thing to do was to get up out of my bed. The thing to do was to just get out and run.

An ancient tree was about to fall in the forest.
The children sensed that it was about to make a sound.

Rideau Hall in Ottawa. Governor General's Residence. That singing group is all decked out in suits.
A dignified man shaking hands with a boy in bloody shorts.
I can tell that Daryll's embarrassed to be standing here in his dirty shorts. It's Ottawa – the Governor-General's Residence. The photographers are here and the TV cameras. Look at me, everybody! Look at the dirty shorts! Take a good look at the artificial leg! Want to see how it works? This is how you run across Canada! This is what you do to make a difference! We're raising funds for Cancer research, everybody! A dollar from every Canadian will make a difference! It's the only way we'll ever get cancer licked! The Governor-General enters the room. The newsmen all come alive. Darrell and me at the front of the line. The cameras start their clicking. Bowing my head to the Governor-General. We both shake hands and smile. Welcome to Rideau Hall. This will be seen by every Canadian. The Governor-General and Darrell and me in our dirty shorts.

"The fundraising powers of Terry Fox are going through the roof. Though returns were modest in the five eastern provinces, now that Terry is known as a

Canada-wide celebrity, what once seemed like wishful thinking – a dollar from every Canadian for cancer research – is now looking to be well within Terry's reach."

Running through morning fog.
Seeing double and feeling dizzy.

Phoning a lady's daughter to talk about cancer.
A leg of straps, steel, gears and fibreglass.
Fires burning in a desolate landscape.

"It's always a battle for space in a Toronto newspaper. At first, I had to fight to get Terry a few lines of ink. And then suddenly he exploded – kicking footballs, throwing out baseballs, chatting with the Prime Minister, shaking hands with the Governor General – posing for pictures with Daryll Sittler and Bobby Orr. Suddenly he was famous. Suddenly everything he did was guaranteed to be featured in the morning papers and on the evening news. There's always an interesting question in our business – is it news because it happens or is it news because it's in the newspapers and on TV? The grimacing face, the sweaty curls, the awkward gait as he braved those lonely miles – people couldn't get enough. From a boy running unnoticed on a string of rural highways to the most famous image-producer in all of Canada. Now he was running in our hearts and in our minds. As soon as Terry was thought to be news, he was front-page news."

Two kinds of cake on a plate and a cup of coffee.
Parliament buildings perched above a river.
A hay-wagon filled to the brim with bales.

"He'll always be running along a Canadian highway."
"He'll always be running his race for the suffering kids."

Reabsorbed into the mantle - people in so much pain - the gods who were on your side - perfect weather near the end - take you off your task - a reminder of blood and bone - why doug doesn't just leave - a story-teller asking - second-largest country - what will come to pass.

One day, I told my mother that I was going to make the run. I thought that she would be the first to believe in me. She told me that she didn't want me to go.

My dad never said too much. He knows me and I know him. He told Mom she couldn't stop me if she tried.

Aside from the family, I didn't tell anyone about my plans. They'd be thinking: "You can't even call that running – more like two hops and a stride. And you're the guy who's going to run five thousand miles?"

"I must tell you a story," the story-teller said,
"But I don't know whether to use 'I' or 'we'."

Running between Charbot Lake and Mountain Grove. The aches and pains don't seem so important. Nice to have these cheering crowds.
Reporters interviewing the members of a waiting crowd.
Not one x-ray since Vancouver. Skipped every one of them on the road. Once I was cured of cancer I didn't need the doctors. Knew that my cancer would never come back. A disability is just a speed-bump. A disability can slow you down but it can't stop you. It's just a bully on your way to school. It's trying to make you disable yourself. It's trying to undermine everything you're trying to be. You have to stare it right back in the face. You have to tell the bully, This is going to be the day I conquer you!

Hurtling down through the bowels
of a dark well.

Asking the Prime Minster to run with me.
Smearing suntan lotion on to ease the sunburn.
People lining the streets of Oshawa all the way.

Life can't get any worse.
This thought kept tumbling through his mind.

"This involved a large-scale amalgamation of most of the Earth's continental plates about a billion years ago into a super-continent which geologists call Rodinia."

You –
a Siamese twin.
Sharing a nightmare with your brain.

Is cancer as famous as Terry Fox?
Do you speak for cancer or does cancer speak for you?
Is celebrity a wolf or is it a dove?

Running between Madoc and Marmora. Can't wait to get to Toronto. The population, media and financial centre of Canada.
A runner in sunshine with fluffy white clouds and a clear blue sky.
It's really great here in Ontario. Every town and every village has a

crowd and signs and people waiting to greet me and give to the cause. It was tough in the first five provinces. Some of the stops were perfect. – School band lining the sidewalks. – Runners jogging alongside of me. – A cheque for the money they'd collected. – Everything I'd hoped for. But in some of those places they never heard of me. People would stop along the sidewalk and stare. The worst was when drivers would offer me a ride. I got so tired of trying to explain. – Running for cancer! – Don't want a ride! Now everybody knows what the run is all about. Looks like everything's going to be fine from here on in.

Chapter 7

Running between Bowmanville and Oshawa. Toronto straight ahead. Population, media, finance. Ontario is the centre of it all.

A crowd of people behind a barricade waving and smiling.

The whole meaning behind the run is coming alive. The newspapers, the television networks, the branches of the Cancer Society. The local politicians and even the Prime Minister and the Governor General of Canada. Everybody is getting behind the run for Cancer. People are coming out of their houses and standing on the roads and streets to cheer and wave as I run by. The Provincial Police are providing an escort and collecting money in their hats. There's a baseball game and some rallies at city halls in the towns ahead. Whole schools of kids are lining all the routes. It's a long way from running in the dark at five o'clock.

No one is immune.

Bus drivers collecting money from their passengers.
Reading the newspapers from back home in British Columbia.
A Peewee baseball team holding out a hat with six dollars.

Anybody can get cancer.

"The collision built a gigantic mountain belt that ran northeast-southwest across eastern North America, with mountains probably rivalling the Himalayas in scale, stretching across Québec, Ontario south of Sudbury and down the eastern half of the continent to Texas."

I could get it again.

Do you hear the voices calling out your name?
Do you realize the place you hold in their hearts?
That some of them say that you have changed their lives?

A shopping mall in Oshawa. Can't believe the size of the crowd. A tremendous blast of applause.
A handsome teenager with a microphone entertaining a crowd.
I turn and shout to Doug. Wonder who they're waiting for? Doug smiles and shouts right back. – It's you! – They're waiting for you! People start to move towards us. Reaching out and shaking my hand. Teenagers asking me for autographs. Mothers saying they wish me well. Organizers making a space and moving me close to the fountain. Helping me climb up onto the ledge. The crowd filling the foyer. Stretching right back to the doors. Of course, it's television! They've been seeing me on TV! I didn't know so many teenagers watch the news. The organizers quiet things down and I say a few words. I turn my back so they can see what it says on my shirt. Please Donate for Cancer Research. Who would have thought that there would be this kind of response?

"Film crews and reporters are recording the epic run of Terry Fox as he makes his way across Ontario, as public enthusiasm for information about the gallant young man who is running for the cause of cancer research is showing no signs of having reached its peak."

"He's running all over Ontario,"
"Putting on hundreds of extra miles."

"Signs and symptoms caused by cancer will vary depending on which parts of the body are affected. Some general signs and symptoms which are associated with, but are not specific to, cancer, include fatigue, a lump or area of thickening which can be felt under the skin, weight changes, including unintended loss or gain, skin changes, such as yellowing, darkening or redness of the skin, sores that won't heal, or changes to existing moles, changes in bowel or bladder habits, persistent cough or trouble breathing, difficulty swallowing, hoarseness, persistent indigestion or discomfort after eating, persistent, unexplained muscle or joint pain, persistent, unexplained fevers or night sweats, and any unexplained bleeding or unusual bruising."

"You wonder what you can give him. Sure – a donation. We all did that. But you're standing on the sidewalk. And here he is, coming along, and you're thinking so many thoughts that you think you'll explode. Like my father's dying of cancer. He lives in the cancer ward. They keep giving him radiation. I know you went through it too. And there's dozens of people on the sidewalk. Everybody has a story to tell. Maybe all of them know about cancer. Maybe that's why everyone's here. So suddenly he's right in front of you. It all goes by so fast. You wave and call out 'Hello'. Everybody does the same. 'We're all with you Terry!' 'Keep it up Terry!' 'Keep going Terry!' That's about all anyone can think of. He gives a little wave back and then he's gone. I told my dad that I'd seen him. He'd been watching it on the TV. They were both alone that night in their separate rooms."

A traffic jam on a highway stretching for miles.
A hot dog with catsup, relish and mustard.
Humidity that makes it hard to breathe.

The sun is the sun - where the marker was - make the numbers bow down - see canada and die - doesn't have an ending - just plain terry fox - people inviting us into their homes - a desolate landscape - nothing you need to fear - pulling a curtain between us.

I'd already played a lot of wheelchair basketball. That had strengthened my shoulders and my arms. But it didn't really do much for my leg.

The first time I ran in a race, my artificial knee broke right in half and I went flying through the air and landed on the ground. A double amputee beat me to the finish line and whooped as he waved his victory crutch and then he turned and looked right back at me.

I started running at night. Didn't want anyone to see me. I wanted to get to a point where I could really run strong with my artificial leg.

"What a wonderful winter morning," the father said to his son.
"Look at the way the sun is sparkling on the snow."

Running between Ajax and Pickering. A big cancer rally scheduled for the Scarborough Civic Centre.

A bus driver collecting money from his passengers.

I had some questions when I started. – Was I going to attract much attention? – Raise much money for cancer research? – Would I be able to run a marathon a day? I had nightmares the first few nights. – What if I ran all the way across Canada and nobody knew? – What if I drove myself to exhaustion and had to stop? I knew myself and I knew the road. I knew the weather and I knew the terrain. What I didn't know was the people and what they would think of what I was doing. So I was running for cancer research. – Why should anybody pay attention? – What if I ran all the way across Canada and nobody noticed? – What if I ran all the way across Canada and nobody cared?

"The size of the crowds has been overwhelming as Terry Fox makes his way across the Province of Ontario on his gruelling Marathon of Hope run across the entire length of Canada. The thousands of well-wishers who have thronged to meet him in such places as the Scarborough Civic Centre and the Toronto City Hall are expressing their support for the cause which Terry has come to represent."

Fighting the pain in my upper chest.
Taking a nap to fight off exhaustion.

Classes sending me their artwork in an envelope.
A mountain that never seems to move.
Telling the newspapers that none of the money is for me.

"I had to get back to the office. And here I was sitting in my car. A grown man sitting and crying. That's what it did to me. I went more as a curiosity. I'd read about him in the newspaper. I was working right downtown. Something to tell the kids that night at supper. There was talk of them getting out of school but it didn't work out. Anyway, I drove to where I knew I'd be able to see him. Almost close enough for me to reach out and touch. There was a crowd gathered to watch him. I stood on the sidewalk beside my car. Terry was running through the intersection. Then one guy started to clap. Then more started to clap and we all joined in. There was a grim look on his face. Concentration on the task. You could tell he was glad to be there. Just a hint of a smile and a nod. I didn't think I would be affected but I was. So that's why I just sat there and cried in the car. Next day, I took the kids out of school, phoned the boss to say I wouldn't be there, and drove us all to the next town to see Terry run."

A yappy little dog who threatens to bite.
Cows lazing under the branches of a tree.
An ancient oak tree standing alone in a grassy field.

"One of those people who leaves an imprint on a culture."
"He'll be an image in our thoughts for a long time to come."

Moment has been buried - entirely different person - a malignant inner-disease - the children sensed - a candle with a flame - some kind of relief - deciding to wear my shorts - phoning a lady's daughter - who i am and why i'm here - so hard to explain.

Running was hard – really hard. It took everything I had. I would come back completely exhausted from a very short run.

I figured it had to be in the rhythm. One artificial and one good leg. The only way to get into a rhythm was to put on the miles.

Then finally I had a breakthrough. I passed two people who were jogging and they both had two legs. How could those two possibly know what I felt inside?

On Tuesday the mountain was there.
Dried by sunlight; soaked by rain.
It looked as if the mountain had not moved.

Running along University Avenue in Toronto. A beautiful July afternoon. Daryll Sittler running beside me. People lining the sidewalks and waving.
A crowd of people cheering as celebrities run by.
People are starting to see me as a star. People shouting out my name. Terry! Terry! Terry! Wanting my autograph. Wanting to touch me. Hey, I'm not hitting any home runs! Not throwing any touchdowns! Not putting pucks in the net! I'm not doing this to be a celebrity! I'm not trying to be rich and famous! I'm doing this to beat cancer! I'm doing this because cancer can be beaten! Everybody's cheering, but I'm wondering what they think they're cheering for.

"Erosion removed some twenty kilometres of the crust over the next 100 million years, so that when a great invasion of the sea began about 600 million years ago the landscape was almost flat."

How many hours have some of them waited to watch you run by?
How many letters and cards have been sent to your home in BC?
Is this developing into something that's bigger than you?

"The cave of the green-god Pan. It appeared out of nowhere in front of Phidippides and blocked his path. And now he stood and stared at the green-god himself. A man if you looked at his torso; a goat if you looked at his thighs; the only gleam of his godhood was in his eyes. 'Welcome to my preserve. I didn't mean to startle you. A slight delay in your run back to Marathon. It will allow you to catch your breath. I have watched you fighting the terrain, your thirst, the heat. Your despair is perhaps the greatest impediment you face. You stumble on the fragments of the failure of your hopes. When your mission resumes, you will run on a smoother path.' "

Hamlin - Saint André - Saint-Leonard Parent - Saint Leonard - Sainte-Anne-de-Madawaska - Grande Isle - Riviere Verte - Madakaska - Edmonston - Moulin-Morneault - Degelis - Riviere-Creuse - Témicouata-sur-le-Lac - Cabano - Whitworth - Saint-Antenin - Riviere-du-Loup - Saint Patrice - Saint-Germain - Kamouraska - Saint-Pascal - Saint Phllipe-de-Néri - Riviere-Quelle - La Pocatiere - Sainte-Louise - Saint Aubert - Monmagny - Berthier-sur-Mer - Levis - Quebec City - Saint Apolonaire - Saint-Flavien - Joly - Val-Alain - Saint-Louis-de-Blandford - Daveluyville – Saint-Cyrille-deWendover - Drummondville - Saint-Germain-de-Grantham - Sainte-Helene-de-Bagot - Saint-Liboire - Saint Hyacinthe.

"His reception in Scarborough and Toronto marks the two thousand one hundred and ninetieth mile for Terry Fox in his bid to run across the entire length of Canada in aid of cancer research."

"I can easily see myself going out for a jog on my seventieth birthday. Or even my eightieth. All of us Foxes seem to live for a good long time."

Toronto City Hall. Can't believe the size of the crowd. Daryll Sittler calms the crowd and gives a speech.
Two athletes receiving the cheers of an adoring throng.
All about me and how my run is an inspiration. But he doesn't forget the kids. I knew he wouldn't. He gives me his all-star sweater on behalf of all the kids who are suffering from cancer. He talks of how blessed he's been and how important it is to give back. And how the kids who are suffering from cancer deserve our best. It's almost more than I can believe. Can't wait to get back to BC. To talk to dad about how we were watching when Daryll Sittler scored ten points that night for the Leafs. Glad to hear the speakers all talking about the need for fund-raising. It's the only reason we're here. Telling the crowd to clap for themselves. I'm just here to raise awareness! You're the Marathon of Hope! You're all involved in this run! The Marathon of Hope is every person who gives a dollar all the way across Canada!

"Terry Fox has been receiving help from an unexpected quarter. Not only does he have a province-wide police escort, here, for the first time in any province, but many of the officers of the Ontario Provincial Police are collecting money on Terry's behalf as it is being offered by the crowds that line the route."

"He's appearing at two or three rallies every day."
"He never turns down an offer to speak to a crowd."

Adjusting my running style each time I develop a blister.
Trying to stifle my cough in interviews.
A person signing a contract which can be changed.

"Easy for us. We went over to the recreation complex and relaxed and had a few laughs. There was a group of people there and of course they were all interested in Terry. Nobody said it but I had the feeling that they were only putting up with us. Any minute they seemed to feel that Terry would appear – tanned, fit and rested – and regale them with charming stories of the run. So all the time we were sitting there telling them stories and joking, Terry was back in the motel room. He had a bad cough that looked like it wasn't going to go away. And he was exhausted and in pain. So he was fighting off the cough and trying to get some sleep. And there was nothing that we could do to help him. Just leave him alone in an empty dark room with his coughing and his pain. So we stayed in the rec hall and told stories and sipped our cokes. We were tired and wanted to sleep, but we knew we could nod a bit tomorrow in the van. Terry badly needed to sleep because tomorrow he'd be running another marathon."

An outdoor concert in a park.
A boy shooting a puck against a wall.
A field of sunflowers dancing in a breeze.

Trying to shake it off - the end of childhood - world in just one person - always an interesting question - measuring the capacity - both were terry fox - school kids singing - people lining the streets - fight off a cold.

Cold sweats, diarrhea, running against the wall of the wind. Needing replacement parts for my artificial leg. Nothing was going to stop me from making my run.

A lot of people probably thought I was crazy. Quite a few of them cheered me on. More than once the same lady stopped to offer a ride.

One hundred and one days in a row. A day off for Christmas and back at it again. All through Christmas dinner I thought about my run.

"Do the children know the date and time?" someone was heard to joke.
"We could print tickets and bring thousands of people to town."

Thousands of people laughing and cheering. Biggest crowd I've ever seen. Great to be talking to the crowd. There's so much I just have to say.

Autograph seekers pressing against the edge of a stage.

There's something bothering me! Something that hurts me when you cheer! I keep hearing my name – Terry Fox! I'm not doing this run for riches or for fame! I'm doing it for cancer – to raise awareness of what cancer is and what it does and what we can do about it! Thousands of people are suffering from cancer and by giving to the cause we can fund cancer research and find a cure! That's why this marathon is so important! It's much more important than me! Even if I don't get to complete it, it has to go on! We need people who are willing to continue – with me or without me! Whether I make it or not the cancer run has to go on!

"The Terry Fox phenomenon has become Canada-wide as the letters and cards of well-wishers and the cheques and money-orders of financial supporters are being sent, in the name of Terry Fox, to cancer centres all over Canada. The young Canadian runner has even been made the subject of a segment on an American news report."

Telling the others to never talk about my heart.
Telling a reporter that I never – ever – dream.

Worrying about the runners who run too close to me.
Twenty or thirty cars behind me waiting to pass.
Thousands of people at the park in London, Ontario.

"Different reporters interviewed him all along the route. Newspapers, TV, radio. He never said much about the media. People in his position learn to be guarded. Publicity can make your whole project or it can tear it all to shreds. Groups of girls started to come around the van when he got famous. One was photographed towelling the sweat off his neck. The picture appeared in a city newspaper. After that picture appeared, he banished all girls from the van. Some reporters he seemed to talk to more than others. With a couple of them he'd hide away and have a very long chat. Most of them, though, he didn't seem to trust. Perhaps he thought they were waiting to pounce. Perhaps they thought he was holding things back. Each of them trying to strike a balance. Things get better or things get worse. They never stay the same. Relationships with the media don't last for life."

A long-haul driver checking the tires on his rig.
A group of workers hoeing corn in endless rows.
A church bell ringing loud and clear.

"His life has meaning for everyone."
"The best of Terry Fox is the best of us."

Just sign the contract - servant of the mind - can't let that be the run - famous image-producer - worth a whole life-time - question that i don't ask him - snow slashing my face - taking rika to the dance - letters that ask for support - in the darkest days.

My leg was taking a pounding. Blisters on my feet; cysts on my stump; bone bruises, callouses, stress fractures, shin splints, ferocious pain in my hip. I would come back from a run with the bucket of my prosthesis dripping blood.

There are thresholds where pain is concerned. It comes in stages and it builds as you run. At times you think that you just can't take any more.

But then you cross a threshold, and your stubbornness equals your pain. The pain retreats to a place in your mind where it doesn't affect your thoughts. It's as if you run past the pain and leave it behind.

"Well, tell us the story first," his listeners all said,
"And we will tell you whether we approve of the ending or no."

Exhibition Stadium. On the shore of Lake Ontario. Lining up with the Blue Jays as the National Anthem is sung.
A young man standing at attention with his hand on his heart.
Tears in my eyes as I sing along with the crowd. Waiting for the standing ovation to stop. Making sure not to bump my nose on the microphone. Telling everybody here that I'm not doing this to be famous! That not one cent of the money will ever go to me! That there's hundreds of kids in the cancer wards who will thank you for your donations! Sitting in the stands and watching the game. Nice to think that my folks are watching it on TV. Everything is working out in ways that I can hardly believe. It's beautiful here in Ontario with the rest of Canada watching. Taking a hotdog. No thanks to a beer. Enjoying myself but wanting to get back on the road.

A miner's hard-hat with a light
would be nice to have.

Biting my tongue as I give an interview.
Pancakes and syrup and pie on the side.
Country music pouring out of the van.

This building has no basement.
This elevator has to stop at the ground floor.

"The Interior Platform Geological Region is named for the area of the Shield which is covered by rocks from the Cambrian to Cenozoic eras; they are largely flat-lying, and this is the main reason for the gentle, low-lying topography that characterizes the landscape."

You – scanning your brain.
Up and down.
Side to side.

What is the bond between you and these people?
Are you asking them for more than they have to give?
Are they asking you for something you can't provide?

Running between Etobicoke and Long Branch. Motorcycle escort from the Province of Ontario. Big receptions planned for Mississauga and Oakville.

A celebrity escorted by police through a cheering crowd.

The mind is just as physical as the body. Just something that you have to work hard to overcome. If you tell yourself you can't – then you can't. If you tell yourself you can – then you can. I've been tired. I've been exhausted. I've had blood pumping out of my stump with every mile. But I told myself that I had to keep on going. I could make two lists. Blood on my stump – agonizing pain – completely exhausted. Better publicity – better fundraising – lots of miles. Just pick the one you want and then go on. For everybody who wants me to run there's someone else who wants me to stop. They'll both be cheering when I stick my leg in the salty brine.

Chapter 8

Running through the streets of Central Ontario. Thousands of people lining the sidewalks. Waving and singing and cheering as I run by.

A boy in shorts and t-shirt standing on a stage.

A rally with hundreds of people. The amount of money keeps going up and up. Two hundred dollars when I arrived here. Standing and listening to the speeches. How the people of Oakville are privileged to have me come here. The numbers on the board changing and changing as the speakers talk. Eight thousand six hundred dollars and moving up. Hundreds of people sharing applause. Invited to the microphone to give my talk.

The pain is always there, but the pain doesn't matter.

Enjoying myself every time I talk to a crowd.
A huge welcome sign at Toronto City Hall.
Demonstrating my artificial leg.

What matters is the incredible feeling.

"In Canada, the Interior Platform includes the prairies of Manitoba, Saskatchewan and Alberta, where the rocks constitute the lower half of the Western Canada Sedimentary Basin."

That's the good that I'm getting out of it myself.

Why is every stride so important?

Why must you run past every single blade of grass?
From sea to sea and everything in between?

Running down the main street of Port Credit. Always keeping my thoughts on the road. Never allowing myself to dream about moments like this.
A roar of applause at a rally in a public park.
Telling them how much it means to me. That other people share my dream. That seeing them here today helps me to know that people are rooting for my success. That people care about the fund-raising. That they care about cancer research. That those kids are not alone in the cancer wards. The numbers keep going up. Every couple of minutes someone changes the board. Eleven thousand two hundred dollars already pledged. And more and more keeps coming in by phone.

"Supporters of Terry Fox are beginning to worry about him. The amazing stamina that he has shown in his gruelling run across what is now his sixth province is being tested to the maximum as he accepts invitation after invitation to appear on behalf of the cause of cancer research."

"Fundraising's going through the roof."
"He's famous all over Canada."

"Start by seeing your family doctor or a general practitioner if you have any signs or symptoms that worry you. If your doctor determines that you have cancer, you will likely be referred to one or more specialists, such as an oncologist, who treats cancer; a radiation oncologist, who treats cancer with radiation; a hematologist, who treats diseases of the blood and blood-forming tissues; and perhaps a surgeon, who performs surgery to remove cancerous tissue."

"We were standing on the street corner. Me and Greg and his shiny new bike. He was really learning to ride it well. The cancer man said that Terry would be running along that route. So I thought that maybe Greg could just ride along beside Terry for maybe a block or two. I hoped he could keep his feet on the pedals. I hoped no potholes would get in the way. I'd be running too, so I could catch him if he started to tip over. It would be so good for Greg. Just to see Terry. Just to say hello. To run along beside someone like Terry for just a little while. Just a little inspiration. Just to see how someone with cancer was getting along. Not so much that he'd grow up to be like Terry. Why think of growing up at all? Just keep the pain away from the thoughts and just think for today."

A group of friends at a backyard barbecue.
A football game with sixteen thousand fans.
A farmer slinging a bag of seed in a pickup truck.

What has transpired - some bad news and some good news - tortoise won the race - i must tell you a story - i won't be here forever - kids playing road hockey - biting my tongue - deciding to have a vote - keeps going on and on - serious for a while.

As far as relationships go, I didn't have many close ones. I could count them on the fingers of my hands. Most of my friendships came to me through sports.

My family has always been at the centre of my life. My mom and dad, my brothers and my sister. I don't see how anyone could replace my family for me.

Would 'relationships' include people I admire? The kind of people I admire are mostly coaches who like to work with younger kids. Kids on sports teams; kids in the cancer wards.

"My eyes have not beheld such wonder," the father said to his son.
"Since your mother was alive and we were poor."

Running down the main street of Oakville. Making the runners keep up a good pace. I came here to run!
A tired boy nodding in sleep at the back of a van.
Long, long days in Southern Ontario. Trips in the van to speak in nearby towns. People waving, people smiling, people in tears. Volunteers passing buckets through the crowds. Trying to keep up the pace of the running. Exhausted by going to every town. Running down the main street. – Shaking hands. – Signing autographs. – Telling my story. – Asking for money for cancer research. – Back in the van. – Supper and sleep. – Up early next morning and back out on the road.

"It is easy to forget, as we listen to Terry Fox address the enthusiastic crowd behind us, that Terry has already run a marathon today, and that tomorrow he will arise at four o'clock in the morning, while most of us are still in bed, and run another marathon before beginning an afternoon and evening of appearances and speeches to even more cheering supporters."

Running down the main street and honking the horn.
Hugging Darrell when he arrives to join the team.

Lost toenails, bone bruises, aching hip.
A backyard barbecue in St. Marys.
Cheeseburger, french fries, milkshake, apple pie.

"Funny how there's a moment when you know you've turned a corner and you know you're never – ever – going back. We were in the van after a rally and there were hundreds of people who were there. And they were shouting 'Terry! Terry! Terry!' And yet – for me – maybe for Terry too – it was when we saw these newspapers on the sidewalk where there was a vendor. And they had a picture of Terry. Curly hair. Rippling muscles. Gorgeous tan. He was standing up on a stage, giving a speech, and the headline just said 'Terry!' and that was all. Maybe the lighting, shining behind him like a halo. Maybe the hands reaching towards him for just a touch. And it all came together at that moment. A popular movie star. A famous singer. A Greek god. Somehow the picture and the headline said it all."

> *A teenaged girl taking her horse over the jumps.*
> *An old lady pulling a cart filled with groceries.*
> *A chainsaw snarling against a tree.*

"His life has meaning for everyone."
"The best of Terry Fox is the best of us."

Need only one leg - ignore the giant - pressing his hand against his chest - one mile at a time - learned to ignore - still free in your mind - wonder who you are - mind like two steel traps - in the presence of a giant - just be terry fox.

I got close to Rika for a while. She used to come over to the house and help me with my homework. If I was going to be serious about the run, I knew I couldn't have a close relationship with a girl.

So I had to ask myself: who could put up with me on a five thousand mile run across the entire country? And who could I put up with for the same five thousand miles? My brother Darrell was out, so I had to try to think of someone else.

Doug and I had been friends since we were kids; in almost every sport, we kept finding ourselves on the same teams. Doug was about the only person outside the family that I could even think of to help on the run. I didn't tell him for a while, but in my mind, I kept rehearsing how I was going to break the idea to Doug.

> *On Wednesday the mountain was there.*
> *Morning sunshine; evening shade.*
> *It looked as if the mountain had not moved.*

Running down the main street of Ancaster. People waving and cheering and clapping. What's pain when you're feeling so happy?
A little girl pointing to blood on a runner's shorts.
Some of these people give me their sympathy but I don't want it. People

think I'm going through hell but I'm not. They see the blood on my shorts or they see the pain in my face and they think I'm in agony. Maybe I am going through hell – some days I think I can't go on – but the other part is that I'm doing what I want. Every dream I've had about the run is coming true and that's what makes it all worthwhile for me. A dream is something you have to pay for. I pay with every drop of sweat. I pay with every drop of blood. There's no other thing in the world I would rather be doing.

"It extends northward down the Mackenzie Valley and then eastward across the Arctic Platform, the belt of Arctic Islands lying south of the Northwest Passage."

Why are people chanting your name?
What do they see when they look at you?
Why does everyone think of you as a brother or a son?

"The green-god Pan spoke to Phidippides. Phidippides panted and listened in awe. 'Dead dreams can be very painful. They haunt; they taunt; they mock. I have good news; I have double-good news. Draw near and I will tell you what will come to pass. First, for Athens, the city which you serve. Your people have been neglecting me – the surge of the Persians has been the result – but this reversal I am willing to grant as a boon: if Athens will promise to celebrate, forever on into the future, the green-god Pan, with sacrifices and torch-lit races, the Persians will be thrown back into the sea. And as for you Phidippides, I have taken note of you. You are a person who toils for no reward. Give all that you have to this race that you must run. To you I will grant release from the runner's toil.' "

Sainte-Madeleine - Boucherville - Montreal - Sainte-Rose - Sainte-Thérese - Blainville - Saint-Jérome - La Chute - Marelan - Grenville - Hawkesbury - L'Original - Alfred - Plantagenet - Clarence-Rockford - Cumberland - Gloucester - Ottawa - Kanata - Stittsville - Black's Corners - Boyds - Innisville - Drummond Centre - Perth - Ungava - Charbot Lake - Mountain Grove - Elm Tree - Kaladar - Hungerford - Actionolite - Madoc - Marmora - Havelock - Norwood - Peterborough - Fraserville - Dranoel - Manvers - Leskard - Kirby - Orono - Clarington - Newcastle - Bowmanville - Oshawa.

"In running into the heart of Southern Ontario – here in London – Terry Fox has accumulated two thousand three hundred and fifty-seven miles in his cross-Canada quest to raise funds for cancer research for the Marathon of Hope."

"Seems like a good long time ago, now, when I had that cancer scare. Seemed pretty serious for a while. I fought off the cancer the way you'd fight off a cold."

Running down the main street of Brantford. A little problem with my thigh, but I can live with it. The thigh gets bigger as I run but the bucket doesn't. Maybe I need to invent a flexible artificial limb.

A group of people sharing a family feast.

Feeling hyper about everything that's happening. A lot going on in the next few days. My parents have joined me in Toronto. My brother Fred came for a surprise. Nice meal at a downtown restaurant with everyone there. A celebration of how the run has gone so far. I've run over two thousand miles. Collected pledges of a quarter million dollars. I know that things are going to go well from now on. I'll have an escort all the way across Ontario. A lot of doubters when I started but I shook them off. Lots of people told me that the whole thing was impossible. Well I'm here now and they can't take that away.

"Mechanical difficulties seem to be plaguing Terry Fox as he continues his epic run. The new artificial leg which he received only days ago has been sent back for repairs and adjustments and the old one – the one which was pinching his stump – has been called back into temporary duty."

"Well the fame hasn't gone to his head."
"He's just the same as the day that he started this run."

Running hundreds of extra miles in Southern Ontario.
A tortoise praying for help in tomorrow's race.
Dumping catsup down the back of Darrell's pants.

"He wanted certain things on the shirt. He'd thought about it for quite a while before we talked. People were starting to show up and meet him with shirts that they'd had made. 'Way to Go Terry.' 'We're with You Terry.' Things like that. His thoughts were pretty precise. 'Can you do a map of Canada? That's the point I'm trying to make. I want that on the front. And also on the front, in lettering as big as you can make it, 'The Marathon of Hope'. That's what I call the run. Both the map and 'The Marathon of Hope'. And on the back will be the thought that I want to leave them with. They'll remember what it says on the back of my shirt. 'Give to the Cancer Society'. Big letters again and nothing else. I've seen a lot of shirts that are so cluttered you can't even read them. The best ones are the ones you can read at a glance.' "

Sunbathers on towels spread on a beach.
Ducks floating on a pond with lily pads.
A machine laying pavement on a street.

Worst is behind you - all i have in my head - the poster-boy for cancer - measured in drops of blood - something from every person - a grinning teenager posing - an alarm-clock lighting a silhouette - the air and the rock and the road - how important this was - one person in the world.

People were always trying to get me to worry about my health. Always suggesting that I go for a checkup or take a rest. If I was going to make this run, I knew I'd have to ignore the state of my health.

People told me to take it easy. People told me I was getting obsessed. I had to give up most of my friends; I found I had to block them out. I had to eliminate everything that I thought would hold me down.

Relationships would have been fine if it hadn't been for the run. The preparations took all of my energy and my time. I just felt that if I was going to dedicate myself to doing something at the highest possible level, I had to learn to rely on just myself.

"Let the old tree die alone," someone was heard to say.
"Trees are dangerous when they fall in the forest."

Running down the main street of Paris. Who wouldn't want to live here? Every town I run through, I'd like to stay.

An office worker sticking pins on a highway map.

I know the War Amps mean well. They've given me support right from the beginning. Gave me my artificial leg and had it repaired every time it broke down along the route. They're having a new one made by a guy who thinks he can improve on what I have now. But I wish they wouldn't talk to the press. And they never should have set-up all these x-rays in these towns I'm passing through. I'm the only one who knows what it's like to be out here on the highway, pounding along on one leg for mile after mile. When people help they should know when to help and when to let things go. Just the artificial leg is all I need and then leave me alone. Don't be telling the press that you think I'm doing myself harm.

"That the publicity for the Marathon of Hope has been overwhelming and that the fundraising for the run has been more than could possibly have been expected is certainly reassuring for those who speak on behalf of Terry Fox. Quietly though, his supporters wonder whether the young runner is not taking on a schedule that is slowly draining away his precious reserves of stamina."

Enjoying the sun on my face as I move along.
Collapsing from exhaustion in the van.

Interviewed for a segment on American TV.

A father and son looking through a window.
An article about a one-legged runner in the New York Marathon.

"Oh Terry had a temper all right. He could be ferocious when he didn't get his way. But – to give him credit – he wanted everything to be perfect for the run. And those early days left scars – I know they did. Running all alone through blizzards, blistering heat and freezing rain. Running through a town with nobody out to meet him. Making his cancer speech to three or four people – the mayor and a clerk and a couple of janitors. That wore him down in the early days of the run. So there was a toughness that was Terry – call it a bitterness if you like – that lingered on inside him somehow – he was human after all – even when he was greeted by cheering crowds and high-school bands. But he never let it show itself in public. He kept it for himself and the guys in the van."

Two old fellows having coffee at a restaurant.
A young girl practicing a violin on a porch.
Construction workers taking a break for lunch.

"There's a media frenzy around this curly-haired boy."
"People will carry him on their backs from here to the coast."

I've only had one dream - end of childhood - the best thing i could do - something you can't provide - a pernicious spreading evil - the only face he could manage - at one with my clan - dwell on the worst - hearing every word - to eliminate everything.

The only people that I let myself think about was the cancer victims. I was saved because of cancer research. More money for cancer research meant that we could save more of those people in the cancer ward.

That was what it amounted to. I was saved by cancer research. More research and we would be able to save more lives.

This is what I was thinking as I ran. There are twenty-four million people in Canada. I'll ask every Canadian to give one dollar for those kids in the cancer ward.

"But it doesn't have an ending," the story-teller said.
"All I can tell you is how the story has gone so far."

Running down the main street of Falkland. Refusing to change my shorts before I run through town.
The raw and bleeding stump of what once was a leg.
I'm sure there's nothing wrong. People are starting to say that there is

but I can't let myself listen to them. If I did I'd still be back in Nova Scotia. That's where they started to cry and whine and bleat. So my stump is bleeding? – So what? – It always has. So the stump is changing shape? – Probably is. It's getting stronger with every mile. – Muscles grow. So they're worried about proper flood-flow. – With all the exercise I'm getting they think I'll get better blood-flow lounging around in bed?

Failing that –
at least a candle
with a flame.

Talking to TV reporters at 4:30 in the morning.
An acolyte learning to focus his attention.
Thousands of people in Nathan Phillips Square.

If there was one, what would it be?
Musty storerooms, cold and damp?

"An area underlain by largely flat-lying Paleozoic sedimentary rocks also extends from Southwestern Ontario, down the St. Lawrence Valley and across the Gulf of St. Lawrence, through Anticosti Island to westernmost Newfoundland."

You –
measuring the capacity
of your skull.

A man whose been strengthened by crippling blows?
A man who has taken the worst and refuses to lie down?
A man who's been beaten down but rises to fight again?

Flying back to Toronto from Niagara Falls. Occasional breaks between the clouds. Watching the shoreline of Lake Ontario. Like a model on a table-top.
A passenger sharing a seat with an artificial leg.
A one hundred dollar cheque from the city of Niagara Falls. The mayor and a couple of councillors. A city with thousands of people. Thousands of tourists enjoying the Falls. The flight from Toronto was a complete waste of time. Too much agony for a hundred dollars. Too much pain for a cheque and a handshake. I want every Canadian to give a dollar to cancer. That's the only way we can fight it. If all I am is another celebrity then all these miles have gone to waste. They tell me I should stick around Toronto as long as I'm getting publicity. – This is the centre of finance and media. – This is the place where you make

the most noise. – Don't leave Toronto until you milk it for all it's worth. Time is passing. The winter is coming. There's a lot more miles still to go. All I really want to do is get out and run.

Chapter 9

Running down the main street of Etonia. Plenty of fund-raising but very little running.

Children smiling for the camera in a cancer ward.

Caught in a whirlpool in Southern Ontario. – Take the van to a city. – Run down the main street. – Meet the mayor and speak at a rally. – Run through another city the next day and do it again.

I'm running for the faces in the cancer clinic.

Chowing down in a restaurant.
A group of gods deciding to have a vote.
A fellow who made a donation in three separate provinces.

Some of the faces have brave smiles. Some have given up smiling.

"Within the Canadian Shield thin remnants of the same sedimentary cover occupy the Hudson Bay and Foxe Basins."

I'm going to take myself to the limit for this cause.

Why don't you sign an endorsement contract?
Why not logos on your shirt and shorts and shoes?
Have you any idea how rich you could become?

Running down the main street of Gobles. Winter is coming on. Looking forward to getting out on the road again.

A group of goofy teenagers having a food-fight.

I guess I should smile more often. People come up to me and shake my hand and ask for my autograph and thank me for what I'm doing as if it was some kind of super-human ordeal. Some of them seem to think it's a nightmare for me to be running all day long, but I love what I'm doing. I'm enjoying myself more now than I was when I was drifting along on two legs. I didn't know what I wanted. – Didn't know what I could be. – Didn't know what kind of future I was going to have. Now the road is right here in front of me. I wake up every morning and I know what I'm going to do and I also know why. People should come around in the evenings, when we're goofing around in the restaurants or in our rooms. People wouldn't feel so bad if they could see me smile.

"Terry's reception in Toronto has been pretty-much of a coronation. Media-savvy commentators say that such a phenomenon fails to suggest a comparison within living memory, as such an outpouring of support for a public figure from usually-reserved Canadians is almost unprecedented."

"I think he's wearing himself too thin."
"Not a fund-raiser where he doesn't make an appearance."

"Cancer diagnosis begins with a thorough physical exam and a complete medical history. Laboratory studies of blood, urine, and stool can detect abnormalities which might indicate cancer. When a tumour is suspected, imaging tests such as X-rays, computed tomography, magnetic resonance imaging, ultrasound, and fiber-optic endoscopy examinations help doctors to determine the cancer's location and size. To confirm the diagnosis of most cancers, a biopsy will be performed in which a tissue sample is removed from the suspected tumour and studied under a microscope to check for cancer cells. "

"So here he was in Ontario. I'd just got back here from Prince Edward Island. We'd heard about him down there. I shied away from going to see him. Hoped that others would, but not me. My mother had recently died of cancer. That's an awful thing to have to go through. And now here's this boy running for cancer. One end of the country to the other. I agreed with what he was doing. Best thing anyone could have done. He got everyone thinking of cancer. People were talking about it at work. But still, I felt a little too close. My mother just passing and all. I had to keep my thoughts at a distance. Now I hold that boy in awe. Wish now that I'd gone to see him. Called out 'thank you' as he passed. But the thought of cancer was just too painful, what with my mother just dying and all. Still I wish I'd gone and called out to him as he passed."

A pickup baseball game in a vacant lot.

A hamburger with french fries and a coke.
A waterwheel creaking slowly beside a mill.

One leg and a pair of shorts - find out what you're made of inside - block of ice - everything i know of as me - coughing into a handkerchief - unintended loss or gain - boy with a missing leg - everything in between - all played out - out of the blue - invested in the soil.

I used to look at a map of Canada that I got from a government office downtown. I told them I needed it for a project that I was working on. On the map, all the distances looked pretty small.

Between runs I would plan out a route. I chose the capital cities. Then I drew my lines on the highways in between.

The map didn't show the hills and valleys. The map didn't show the rain and the snow. But I figured I'd faced all the tough stuff right here in BC.

"What to compare it with, I wonder?" the father asked his son.
"The sunlight looks like diamonds on the snow."

Running down the main street of Creditville. I love the restaurants in these little towns. Glass of coke and a cheeseburg sounds good right about now.

A waitress flirting with a handsome curly-haired boy.

No company endorsements. I don't know why I have to keep saying it. Everybody wants to get on the bandwagon. Everybody wants to make a buck. I keep telling them over and over: companies can donate but they won't be allowed to advertise. Some of them are going along with it and some are backing away. People tell me I'm being stubborn. – Share the profit. – We can all make a buck. Well that's it and I'm not going to budge. There won't be any company logos on my shirt or my shorts or my shoes. All they're going to see when they look at my shorts is my blood.

"A lonely figure loping his solitary way along a ribbon of pavement as the dawn comes up over the horizon. The deliberate placing of one leg in front of the other one as he ekes out the miles along a deserted highway. The grimace of pain as he slugs out one more mile despite torturous weather and road conditions. This is the image of Terry Fox that is resonating with Canadians everywhere in this vast country of ours."

Telling my leg jokes to ninety laughing kids.
Getting the joint in my knee repaired at a local shop.

School kids donating all their milk money.
A girl with cancer giving me a rose.

The whole town of Woodstock cheering me on.

"My dad was the organizer and Terry needed his rest. My dad was in a meeting so I was playing outside in the hall. And I was told to be quiet and not to make noise and wake Terry. So I was playing with my toys and making noises without really thinking. I'd make the motor noises for the cars. And this door behind me opened and it was Terry. So I didn't know what to do. I thought my dad would really be mad. But Terry invited me into the room. We sat on his bed and made faces. We were making each other laugh. I'm sure we could have gone on for hours, but suddenly Terry stopped and said 'You'd better get back to the others. Your dad is going to wonder where you are.' I always hoped we'd play again. I didn't know how to ask my dad, and everybody else said Terry needed his rest."

A hand waving goodbye from a train.
Apple orchards coming into ripeness.
A baseball game with a strong breeze from the lake.

"From now on he'll be running in a media glow."
"Millions of dollars are starting to flow towards his name."

The gods who voted against you - only human after all - the mind against the mind - everybody has a story - living on the raw edge - adjustments can be improvised - everything to be perfect - as swift as the hare - heat, humidity, lack of sleep - your name alone.

The whole medical side of this journey is the dark side. It's the side that I don't like to talk about at all. It's the side that everyone else seems to want to know.

I'd be running alongside the water or up a hill. I'd stop to take a drink and catch my breath. Someone would tell me that there were drops of blood on my shorts.

I knew that people wanted to help me. I never doubted that at all. But I couldn't – ever – let them have any influence over me.

On Thursday the mountain was there.
Winter snowfall; summer sun.
It looked as if the mountain had not moved.

Speaking at schools and malls and ball-games. Speaking to hundreds at a time. Hoping they understand what this is all about.
A young man speaking passionately into a microphone.
I don't have cancer! That's what people need to know! I don't have

cancer and I'm running to help the people who do! That's what I'm trying to get through to people! We don't just do things for ourselves! We do them for others! I was selfish until I spent time in the cancer ward! Those voices that I heard changed my life! Now I'm telling everybody what it was like! I'm telling them because I'm the one who knows! Because those kids in the cancer wards can't speak for themselves!

"All of these areas underwent a major invasion of the sea, at some time between about 550 and 450 million years ago, which lasted until late in the Devonian period, about 360 million years ago."

How do you pick and choose from your options?
How do you keep the vision pure?
Never tempted to take a few small perks for yourself?

"Marathon on a pivotal day. A nightmare in brutal sunlight. The Persians fighting fiercely and bravely. Phidippides in the thick of the battle. Bringing water in leather buckets; swinging a hatchet; throwing a spear. Tending a comrade; binding a wound; thinking a prayer. The day wears on and the blood flows freely. Fighting for empire; fighting for home. Which was to be the deeper motive for sticking to task? Piles of dead bodies; the flower of manhood; other treasures in other lands. A full-flank withdrawal; a snarly conference; sailing for home. Drinks for the wounded; counting the dead; watching the Persian fleet sail away from the top of a hill."

Whitby - Ajax - Pickering - Scarborough - Toronto - Etobicoke - Long Branch - Cooksville - Mississauga - Port Credit - Oakville - Bronte - Hamilton - Ancaster - Brantford - Paris - Falkland - Etonia - Gobles - Creditville - Woodstock - Thamesford - London - St. Marys - Stratford - Kitchener-Waterloo - Guelph - Georgetown - Brampton - Niagara Falls - Rexdale - Concord - Vaughan - Nobleton - Schoenberg - Newton Robinson - Barrie - Orillia - Severn Bridge - Bracebridge - Gravenhurst - Allenville - Huntsville - Melissa - Burks Falls - Sundridge.

"Terry Fox has run hundreds of extra miles in Southern Ontario for the purpose of raising funds for cancer research. If his only reason for being here had been to run across Canada by the shortest route, he need not do these extra runs in Southern Ontario."

"I never doubted that I would live. Even in the darkest days. I always knew that I would live for a good long time."

Stopping and speaking in Woodstock and Thamesford. Everybody taking photographs. Everybody shouting my name.

A group of people surrounding a celebrity at a soccer park.

Terry! Terry! Terry! Can't ask them to shout out Cancer! but cancer is the reason I'm here. Wouldn't want them to come and see me and not give a dime. Sometimes I get a little worried. How to keep things separate and not let things get confused? So hard to explain what I'm trying to say. I'm just Terry Fox – the runner! Sure you've seen me on TV, but I'm not a TV star! I'm not doing this for fame or money! Not a penny will go to me! Every dime is for cancer research! I'll go back to Port Coquitlam! I'll go back to things as they were! When this is over I'll just be Terry Fox!

"The cheerful smile and the wave of greeting. The shy acknowledgement of the thunderous applause. The insistence that he is running for cancer victims and not for himself. The heartfelt speech about the need for cancer research and the joking about only wearing out one sock at a time. All of this goes to make up the image that is warming the hearts of Canadians from coast to coast and far into the north."

"Hear he's frustrated here in the south."
"Hear he wants to move on to the north."

Telling everyone that cancer can be beaten
Stress in my back from the twisting of my leg.
Showing my stump with the scars and the sores to the kids in the schools.

"I was there when Terry collapsed. More than once in fact. The heat and humidity got to him. Running in Southern Ontario in summer is pretty tough. Especially tough for a person from the West. And the pain and the coughing were bad. And lots of other things were wrong. You could see him going down-hill. Not when he stood up on those stages. There he was handsome and healthy and proud. But there were things that the people didn't notice. All that running was taking its toll. The stride was getting less purposeful. The chest wasn't breathing as well. All those little things were making it harder and harder to run. It was a super-human effort by a human boy."

Used car lots with hundreds of bargains for sale.
A father and son playing catch in a park.
A mother and daughter shopping for a dress.

What the sage had said - 250 million years ago - wondering what to do - break out of their cage - what you can give him - stretched out on a bed - the physical requirements - turns against itself - choose such a path - what it amounted to.

The dizziness, the extreme fatigue, the double-vision. The enlargement of the left ventricle of my heart. Always wondering what the next set of x-rays was going to say.

The headaches, the cold sweats, the sores, the scabs and the blood. I kept track of these just like I kept track of the miles. I had to be aware of everything about me, but I had to be careful how I thought about what it meant. Drops of blood on my shorts or on my prosthesis meant that there were tougher days ahead; it didn't mean that I shouldn't be planning this run.

There was a battle going on and I faced it every time I went out to run. There was the physical and there was the mental. I never doubted which one was going to come out ahead.

The parents were heard to make pronouncements to the children.
"I can imagine what you would say if it fell on you."

A hotel room in London. Been lying here for an hour but can't seem to sleep. Newspapers on the bed and on the floor. TV giving the news without the sound.

A person staring at a slow-moving ceiling fan.
So I'm tired. So I'm exhausted. So I don't get my sleep. Rain, heat, hills. Lots of humidity here in the south. Doctors and reporters barking like dogs every mile. I'm not going to let them stop me. Make me turn against myself. One mile, one day, one marathon. I'm staying in my groove. Once I get into Northern Ontario things'll be fine.

"All of Canada is taking notice of the lonely one-legged boy who is running for cancer. His curly hair, suntanned face and determined grimace while he is running coupled with his crowd-pleasing smile and earnest pleas for contributions at countless receptions have made him not only the poster-boy for cancer research but the very image of how Canadians see the best in themselves."

Getting better at telling jokes.
Demonstrating my artificial leg.

People crowding around the van.
A young boy fishing beside his grandfather.
Telling a technician to just fix the leg and forget the advice.

"I tried to get him to talk about the future. We were sitting in a hotel room. He looked a little out of place. He was waiting to talk to a whole room full of business executives. I said 'Terry I don't think you realize how big this thing could grow to be. These are some pretty high-profile businessmen. They'll be only too willing to match donations two for one. Once they hear you speak every one of them is going to have stars in his eyes. Millions of dollars can be raised on your name alone. It just has to be nurtured carefully. It needs a process to channel the flow. This whole thing can be just the beginning. It could be gigantic in a very short while.' He just sat there with a grim look on his face. He checked his watch from time to time. You could tell that he was in a lot of pain. He seemed to sense that his body was slowly weakening. He blocked me out like he was pulling a curtain between us. Talk of the future was something he didn't want to hear."

A college student pumping a tank of gas.
A mother weaving braids in her daughter's hair.
A line of cows walking slowly back to the barn.

"Every cause needs a celebrity."
"Every ailment needs a hero."

Going to be okay - to have a plan - poisoning my mood - hurting must stop - sores that won't heal - faces in the cancer clinic - the latest storm of pain - establishing a rapport - didn't have an outlet - everything in the world.

To plan to run on a prosthetic leg; to plan to run a marathon a day; to plan to run every day through the spring and the summer. No wonder everybody told me that I was wrong. The only voice that said I was right was the voice inside.

I never allowed myself to think of myself as disabled. I had a handicap just like anyone would have in golf. All it meant to me was that I would have to work extra hard.

Every day, I would go out and run. Every day, my good leg got stronger. I told myself that all I needed was one good leg.

"Well, tell us what you know," his listeners all said.
"When we have heard it, we can choose that story or no."

Back in Toronto again. Comparing legs with Bobby Orr. The scars on his knees are like a road map.

An older athlete presenting a younger with a Team Canada sweater.

The thing about Bobby Orr is the short career. We'll never know how great he could have been. Could have been the greatest hockey player ever — we'll never know. Probably his greatest feat was playing on two bad knees. The bones would grind against the bones with every stride. I read it in a hockey magazine. But we don't get into that. I show him my stump with the cuts and bruises. He shows me his knees with the stitches and scars. Two pretty banged up athletes having a laugh. We keep it pretty light but I'm thinking all the time. He's the only one who knows. He's the only one who can look into the future and see just how great he could have been. There must have been a day – one single, painful, devastating day – when he knew that he wouldn't be able to play anymore. We shake hands and pose for pictures as the flash-bulbs pop.

Failing that –
what could one wish for?

Good luck swallowing bad luck; bad luck swallowing good.
Figuring out what I want to say on the t-shirt.
Looking for a pile of stones in the morning dark.

Spiders, darkness, rats?
Whips, thumbscrews, a rack?

"As a result a gigantic inland sea developed, probably covering almost the entire continent."

You –
laying charges against yourself
for desertion.

Does what people value in us distort us?
Do we become what people see?
When people look at us do we change before their eyes?

A fancy room in a fancy hotel. Waiting to talk to a bunch of people who want to help.
A board room with a table and gentlemen wearing suits.
This heat is starting to get me. The heat and the humidity of Southern Ontario. I think that's what's making me cough. I'm putting on hundreds of extra miles to raise the funds. I've got to get up north where the air is clean and clear and I can breathe.

Chapter 10

Lying on a bed in a hotel room in Toronto. TV on and dinner on a tray. My artificial leg on a cushy chair.

A young man with his eyes tightly closed.

I've been running all over Southern Ontario. Hamilton, Brantford, Paris, London. I've been running down every main street, giving speeches at city halls, attending receptions in every Legion and every arena. But these short runs are just for show. They don't add up to many miles. I'm supposed to be running a marathon a day. I could have lit out north from Toronto when I came here the first time. The miles aren't going to run themselves. A lot of highway from here to BC. Winter's going to come on soon and I might get caught.

I love what I'm doing.

A freight truck hitting a television van.
Dressing up and taking Rika to the dance.
An ancient Greek runner gritting his teeth.

I'm enjoying myself so much, which is something that other people can't seem to realize.

"In it, some of the earliest invertebrate life forms flourished, including trilobites, brachiopods and corals."

Even though it's so difficult, there is not another thing in the world that I would rather be doing.

Are you a man in search of yourself?
Do you wonder who you are?
Are you chasing Terry Fox mile after mile?

Hotel room in Toronto. Turning the TV off and closing my eyes.
A television screen completely black.
That flight to Niagara Falls was a waste of time. Wish I'd never bothered to go. Just the mayor and a couple of councillors and no one else. A pretty puny cheque when you consider how many tourists were there for the Falls. Invited to pose with the animals. Mentioned passing the hat and they said we couldn't do it. A no fund-raising for charity policy they said. All they wanted was the publicity. Pictures of me feeding the cute baby deer. Told them I wouldn't go if we couldn't raise any funds. Then a long and grumpy flight back to Toronto. Trying to keep myself from feeling so awfully low.

"The Terry Fox Marathon of Hope is leaving Southern Ontario soon and heading north and then west above the vast expanse of Lake Superior. Terry's run through this part of Ontario has been nothing short of phenomenal, as he has been greeted by enormous crowds and the fund-raising aspect of his journey has reached undreamed-of proportions."

"You have to give the kid a lot of credit."
"Started out in the rain and the cold without a dime."

"Once cancer is diagnosed, your doctor will work to determine the stage of your cancer. Your doctor uses your cancer's stage to determine your treatment options and your chances for a cure. Staging tests and procedures may include imaging tests, such as bone scans or x-rays, to see whether cancer has spread to other parts of the body. Cancer stages are generally indicated by Roman numerals – I through IV – with higher numerals indicating more advanced cancer. In some cases, cancer stages are indicated using letters or words."

"Funny thing is I missed him earlier in the day. I was in a restaurant and someone came in and said 'Terry Fox just ran by'. I checked my watch and – geeze – I had to run to get back in time for work. A bunch of us were talking about the Leafs and the usual stuff so I missed him. That evening, after supper, I watched it on TV – the cheering crowds and the mayor and the band and all. He made a speech that really tore at your heart. Then, later that night, I went out to buy a quart of milk. And it was just like in a movie. Or a dream or something. This van pulls up to the curb and the door opens and it's him! He works himself down out of the seat and onto the curb and then he walks in that walk of his across the sidewalk and into the building. No lights, no cameras, no speeches.

Don't know what kind of store or office it was. Getting his leg checked out I guess. It was getting dark and the street was quiet as can be. I stood there for a while and then decided to let him have his privacy, so I moved on. I've just seen Terry Fox, I said to myself. The real Terry Fox – not the one on TV. Just Terry Fox on the empty sidewalk. The thing that struck me was how alone he looked – how tired and how alone."

A lineup at a window to buy ice-cream.
Boys trading baseball cards at a park.
A pop machine on a hot August afternoon.

Need another terry fox - have what it takes - listening to the screams - who could believe - the way the sun is sparkling - super-human ordeal - a large scale amalgamation - trying to stifle my cough - driving myself to exhaustion - everybody told me.

Every day I was getting better. One day I ran thirty miles. I figured the good leg had to be strong enough for two.

I was running up Burrard Mountain. I was paying the highest price. I knew I could run a marathon every day.

Someone told me that soon I'd be ready to run across BC. "Oh, I'm going to do that," I said. "But first I'll do the whole cross-Canada run."

"The sun is the sun and the diamonds are diamonds," the son said to his father.

"While you were asleep I flung them out on the snow."

Hotel room in Toronto. The room is dark but I still can't seem to sleep.
A stack of cancer brochures on a table beside a bed.
Cancer is watching a horror movie at night when you're home all alone. Cancer is being trapped in a well without a glimpse of the sky. Cancer is like lying on a drawer in the morgue with your eyes open. Cancer is like living on death row with no chance of appeal. Cancer is having your palm read and being told you only have a week or maybe a day. Cancer is the ghost who looks like a person in the family photograph. Cancer is all the demons in hell on Hallowe'en.

"Everywhere he goes in Southern Ontario, Terry Fox is drawing enormous crowds. The people have taken him to their hearts and seem to draw great inspiration from the sense of hope in the face of tragedy that Terry has come to represent. Country roads are lined with cars and people and city sidewalks are bursting with crowds who just want to show their appreciation as he continues his run."

Calling the schools and asking if I can come.
Calling the mayors in the towns to let me speak.

Pain from the cysts, no sleep from the heat, no time for myself.
Dropping a post card into a mailbox for the family.
Crying when I think of how Doug puts up with me.

"He just had to get out of Southern Ontario. He was stretching himself too thin. It was really wearing him down. That was just the way it was. It was all his own choice. He was surrounded by lots of help but they could only do so much. He was the one who did all the speeches. He was the one who did all the running. And it was important to him to try to reach out to as many people as he could. He got exhausted but he never got lazy. More than one person tried to talk him into slowing down. Everybody who criticized him – the doctors and the War Amps and a lot of the newspaper writers – all of them tried to get him to ease up on the pace. A lot of them heaved a sigh of relief when he headed up north."

A man painting his windowsills bright blue.
A lady pulling weeds in a flower garden.
A baseball team all licking their ice-cream cones.

"People are literally singing his praises."
"There's even a song on the radio about Terry Fox."

Every desert is a garden - make the numbers dance - somebody opened the door - sharing a nightmare - drifting along on two legs - both alone that night - a different terry fox - absorbed canada into my bloodstream - go from day to day - what i was thinking.

I sat down and wrote a letter. Rika helped me with the words. I never paid a lot of attention in English class.

"I will take myself to the limit." "Somewhere the hurting must stop." "I have to believe in miracles, and I do."

I sent it to the Cancer Society. I sent it to companies galore. "I am going to need a vehicle, running shoes, food and gas."

On Friday he climbed the mountain.
Two more days – a trillion years – infinity.
He was sure now that the mountain would never move.

Hotel room in Toronto. Told the others to leave me alone. Maybe I should call them in and goof around for a while.
A person alone in a room who coughs and coughs.

Cancer is a dull pain in your leg which doesn't seem important. Cancer is blinding headaches, dizzy spells, extreme fatigue and searing pain. Cancer is being eaten alive by your own body. Cancer is going into a room with two legs and coming out with one. Cancer is lying in a bed in the recovery room and hearing the children scream. Cancer is the last thing you would want to experience before you die.

"The limestones that were deposited at this time are well seen in the front ranges of the Rocky Mountains, in the Niagara Gorge and underlying Parliament Hill in Ottawa."

What is the connection between yourself and Daryll Sittler?
What is the connection between yourself and Bobby Orr?
Do you raise your hockey stick when you hear the applause?

"Relief on the Plains of Marathon. The Persians defeated; turning their backs; sailing away. The Athenians exhausted; treating their wounded; counting their dead. Miltiades then spoke; he of the helmet; he of the sword. 'We need someone to run to Athens. To tell the city of our great victory. To tell them their lives have all been spared. To have them prepare the sacrifices and the torch-lit races in honour of the green-god Pan. Are you up for the task, Phidippides? Perhaps another should take your place. You, as much as any, have earned a reprieve.' Phidippides held his hand to his side. 'I am ready to run, my general. I am a man who seeks no reward. Let me be the one to announce that Athens is saved.' "

South River - Trout Creek - Powessan - North Bay - Sturgeon Falls - Warren - Yellek - Beaucage - Meadowville - West Nippissing - Verner - Markstay-Warren - Wahnapitae - Coniston - Sudbury - Whitefish - Nairn Centre - Espanola - Webwood - Spanish - Algoma Mills - Blind River - Iron Bridge - Thessalon - Bruce Mines - Desbarat - Echo Bay - Garden River - Sault Ste Marie - Heyden - Galois River - Harmony Beach - Montreal River Harbour - Agawa Bay - Wawa - White River.

"As much as he is enjoying Southern Ontario, two landmark events await Terry Fox as he prepares to venture into Northern Ontario: he will reach the half-way mark in terms of the length of Canada and he will get to celebrate his twenty-second birthday."

"I really love my job. It has to do with helping kids. As a matter of fact, it's helping kids who've come down with cancer."

Hotel room in Toronto. The only thing that gives any light is the clock.

A person flinging a pamphlet across a room.

I'd have to be pretty selfish to lie there in a cancer ward in the middle of the night and think of myself. I couldn't believe the screams that were coming out of those kids. If I'd been in another ward – with any other kind of ailment – I probably could have listened to screams and thought at least things are going to get better. That the hospital is where the patients come to get cured. But not in the cancer ward. I knew that only a few would get out alive. All I had to do is just glance at those cancer brochures.

"Terry's triumph in Southern Ontario has not been without its drawbacks. There are those who have come to question the enormous burden that Terry has placed upon himself, as he is running a marathon a day and then attending as many as three fundraising events in the hours when his run is completed for the day. There is fear that all of this activity is taking a toll on Terry's health."

"Millions of dollars are pouring in for cancer research."
"He's brought everybody in Canada onto his side."

Running past police cars and film crews.
A little girl who lost her hair from chemo treatments.
A person falling down inside a dark well.

"He wouldn't ride in a limousine. Wouldn't hear of it. He had given a speech one time and he was standing at the curb and this limousine pulls up and the driver comes around and opens the door. And Terry says 'Who's this for?' and someone says, 'You. It's here to take you back to the van.' And Terry says 'I'm not getting in that thing. Isn't there someone who has a car or we could take a taxi.' 'But it's free,' someone says. 'It's like a donation.' 'Doesn't matter,' Terry says as he's standing there on the sidewalk. 'Cleaning ladies count their pennies and send them in to the cancer drive and I'm going to ride around in a limousine?' He was getting a little hot with his people. 'You're all going to have to do a little more thinking. Tell the driver to take it away. I'm not going to ride in that thing. Get a fund-raiser's car or a beat-up old taxi or we'd all of us better start running back to the van!' "

Girls playing hopscotch on a sidewalk.
A lady walking a poodle on a leash.
Bleachers filled with a dozen cheering fans.

One of those miracle breakthroughs - bound to each other - epic enterprise - what i didn't know - helped by a lot of people - fails to suggest a comparison - runners who run too close - no reversing it - all of it is happening to me.

Time to make some final decisions. Who would go with me and who would not? In the end, I didn't really have much of a choice.

As far as my brothers and sister go, Darrell would have been perfect for the run. But Darrell was still in school. Better to stick to the books and get ready for his exams.

My friend, Doug, wasn't sure whether he should come along with me. I told him I needed him to help. I could run all the way across Canada with an artificial leg, but I couldn't drive a camper-van as well.

An ancient tree was about to fall in the forest.
Silently, urgently, the tree rehearsed its first and final words.

Hotel room in Toronto. What time would it be in BC?
An empty bed, as neat as a pin, in a cancer ward.
Cancer is a little boy telling you a story in the cancer ward. Hockey players skating and shooting on his brand-new flannel pajamas. Late at night and the nurses making their final rounds. Lying next to him and listening as he talks. – My dad's going to take me to watch a game when I get better. – Every Saturday night we watch hockey in the rec room. – My mom, my dad, my sister, my grandma and me. – When the team lets in a goal, my grandma always shouts at the TV. Then the lights blink in the ward. – Well, goodnight, he says to you. Then he yawns and slides down into the bed and pulls the covers up close beneath his chin. The last thing he says is – Tomorrow, I'll tell you who's my favourite player. Next morning, the bed is made and he isn't there.

"It is hoped, by many who are close to Terry Fox, that the pressure-cooker of publicity that has been his lot in Southern Ontario will ease as he moves into Northern Ontario, and that his schedule of rallies and receptions will lighten enough to allow him to get some much-needed rest and to concentrate on the completion of his run."

Massaging my stump.
Crying on the phone.

A man building a house to be extra-strong.
Trouble with the air-conditioning in the van.
Feeling like a phony because of Doug.

"I sat down and wrote out a plan. I presented it to Terry near the end of the run. I said 'You've started something big. Bigger than even you could know. Can you imagine an annual run? With everyone running? Raising money that will go towards finding a cure for cancer? In every city and town across Canada? Every Canadian will either be running or making a pledge. The theme will be that cancer can be beaten. All we need is a lot more research. And this will be all inspired by you. They'll all be running in your t-shirts. You'll be running in their hearts. Your dream will spread like wildfire. It will spread around the world. Every year, an annual run. We'll name it after you. The Terry Fox Marathon of Hope.' "

A cool verandah on a hot afternoon.
A dump truck grinding up the hill of a quarry.
A lady offering samples of homemade cheese.

"There'll be runners all over the world with his name on their shirts."
"His name will be mentioned whenever a cure for cancer is found."

I believe in miracles - what seed you have planted - all downhill to vancouver - the pathological condition - a soldier whose role it was - ask those school kids - being attacked by something - lost toenails, bone bruises, aching hip - a person deciding - what is now eastern canada.

It was other people's pain that kept me going. I went back to the cancer ward to say good-bye and tell them a bit about what I was going to do. There wasn't one patient there that I'd known before.

I didn't know much about publicity. I've learned quite a lot since that time. Did some interviews with the local media before I left town.

Then we flew all the way to St. John's, Doug and I. Everything was there, according to promise: the camper-van was bright and shiny and new. Doug asked me the night before, in the hotel room, if I was nervous, but I told him no. Couldn't wait to dip my leg in the salty brine.

I didn't offer the choice of a story," the story-teller said.
"I was wondering whether the story was 'I' or 'we'."

Hotel room in Toronto. Haven't run for a couple of days.
A tray with a glass half-full and some untouched food.
Very few people ever get cured. That's the bottom line. Those kids lie suffering there in the dark and it only gets worse. I was eighteen when I first got cancer. They could have put me in the adult section. But they put me in with the kids. It was easier for me to deal with it. I always felt I'd be okay. But I imagined how a kid must feel. Lying there in the dark. – Why am I all alone? – Why am I in such pain? – Is anybody going to make it stop? All these thoughts went through my mind. I whispered in the dark. I gave those kids my word. I would spend the rest of my life helping those kids.

Hurtling down with a stubby candle

and a tiny flame.

Darrell holding out his hand with a cup of water.
Fries with gravy, baked beans and Black Forest Cake.
Jumping into a ditch to save my life.

Life can't get any worse.
This elevator has to stop at the ground floor.

"Reefs formed by primitive colonial organisms flourished in the area corresponding to present-day Alberta, and became the host for much of the oil and gas that forms the foundation for the modern economy of that province."

You –
looking through your own eyes
from the outside in.

Are you a man running alone through a wilderness?
Are you a man carrying everything he owns?
Or are you a running man with a nation on his back?

Hotel room in Toronto. Cushy bed and big-screen TV.
A man looking out the window of a hotel-room.
Told them I didn't want a luxury suite but they said they didn't have anything else. – Important to stay another day! – Important that you talk to important people! – Southern Ontario is a fund-raising gold mine! – Your time is now! So many things to do. Run a marathon. – Attend a rally. – Give a speech. – Collect some money. – Pose for pictures. – Give an interview. – Adjust my equipment. – Rest my leg. I need to do every one of these things every hour of every day. Not enough time. Not enough energy. Not enough me. How many Terry Foxes do I need to be? Great to be here but can't wait to leave. The publicity's great for the fund-raising but the rest is breaking me down. Just want to head up north. Lots of water, rocks and trees. All I'll have to do all day is just run and run.

Chapter 11

Running between Orillia and Severn Bridge. A stride, two hops and a stride. Running my way out of Southern Ontario.

A small figure running alone among tall pines.

Running free in Northern Ontario. Rocks and trees and waterfalls. Miles and miles of highway and only little towns along the way. Small groups come out to meet me when I run along their main streets. Everybody wants to help as much as they can. It'll be a long way across the north shore of Lake Superior – that's what everyone tells me – but I can take it. Nothing's going to stop me now. Not the distance, the blood or the pain. I'll run through pain and out the other side.

Get to that sign. Get to that corner. Get to that bend.

Tall trees reaching forever on every side.
A ring-master controlling a bunch of numbers.
A newspaper article that cuts like a knife to the heart.

That's all I ever think about.

"At the time the marine invasion of Canada was taking place, the giant continent, Rodinia, was beginning to break up, forming new oceans."

I never let myself think of anything else.

Just the air and the rock and the road?

Just the trees and the waterfalls?

Just a man alone with his thoughts somewhere under the sky?

A parking lot outside a restaurant. Gravenhurst. Doug and Darrell carrying a cake. Bill with a bunch of presents.

A group of young guys goofing around in a parking lot.

My twenty-second birthday. Tried not to think of it out on the road. Life is passing me by so quickly. I want to achieve some kind of accomplishment. I want to reach a meaningful milestone. My sense of urgency is getting stronger every day. But, hey, there's no way I'm going to make an emotional speech. I know these guys too well to let my guard down. A couple of reporters ready to snap a picture. A photograph for all the newspapers and the TV. The Cancer Society probably won't like it. The War Amps won't like it either. But hey, I'm twenty-two. I need a break from all this thinking and this will do. I wait 'til they're close and then I make my move!

"It is inspiring to watch Terry Fox as he runs in Northern Ontario. The hills can be steep, the heat can be stifling, the road can be awfully long, but one senses that Terry Fox has gotten his second wind. He told this reporter that it's all downhill from here."

"The cleaner air will help with the running."

"Pretty soon he'll be half-way."

"Doctors have many tools when it comes to treating cancer. Cancer treatment options include surgery, chemotherapy, radiation therapy, bone marrow transplant, immunotherapy, hormone therapy, targeted blood therapy and clinical trials. Other treatments may be available to you, depending on your type of cancer."

"Terry didn't have any safety harness. You know those machines that people work at where their hands and arms are strapped into a safety harness? It's so you don't get pulled into the machine. So you can make something without your hands getting mangled. That's what most of us wear all our lives. Well, Terry's were removed when he had his cancer and lost his leg. Then the choice was either to retreat from life or to face it bleeding and raw. So Terry made his choice. He made it in the cancer ward where he heard the children screaming. Terry still wanted to make something. He found himself bleeding and raw, but he plunged right into life without restraint."

Miles of water rock and trees.

Sunrise in the morning over a lake.

Lines of cars heading north on a Friday afternoon.

When things go wrong - cannot take a day off - cut short by the call - imprint on a culture - studied under a microscope - adjustments can be improvised - run through pain - giving me a rose - to let things go - all I really want.

I dipped my leg in the Atlantic Ocean. The next drop of salt water was five thousand miles away. I told myself that the next time I dipped my leg in salt water, it would be in the Pacific Ocean.

I told myself that someday the run would end. Cancer could be beaten. The pain would be gone.

I pictured myself in Port Renfrew. Raising my arms in the air and dancing around in the waves. Shouting "Every Canadian was with me on the run!"

"Why so much rock, so much water, so much sky north of Superior?"
The young boy asked his grandfather as they baited their hooks.

Running between Burks Falls and Sundridge.
A group of young friends sharing a drink by the side of the road.
Moving briskly along the highway. Running as smoothly as a machine. Both legs pumping like pistons. Heart pumping smoothly. Hip and ankles free of soreness. Health as good as it needs to be. Doug and Darrell in the van. Water ready at every mile. Crowds of well-wishers and donors waiting ahead. Publicity in local papers and on TV. Putting the miles on my personal odometer. Thoughts of cancer fading away. My mind as clear as a mirror. Thinking of nothing but my own thoughts. Perfect weather, perfect scenery, perfect day.

"Terry Fox's eyes sparkle as he shakes hands along the route and talks to crowds in the small towns of Northern Ontario. Everywhere he goes people know him as a brother and want to shake his hand or merely wave to him as they drop whatever amount of money they can spare into the collection buckets."

Feeling the tiredness growing on me with every mile.
Refusing to say a word when I'm on my breaks.

Money pouring in from all over Canada.
Feeling good about making the high school basketball team.
Trying to toughen Darrell up about the media.

"So who owns Terry Fox? That was the question at a certain point in the run. People would beg to have Terry come and talk to them. Those gymnasiums and recreation halls would be bursting at the seams. After all, Terry was going to run through their town and along their highway. And the media wanted interviews. Not just shot after shot of Terry running along the road. They wanted to know what he was thinking and what he was feeling for their readers and viewers. And they wanted something new every day. And of course, Terry's handlers – the cancer people or the guys in the van – would say 'Of course Terry'll be there. He'd love to be there for the speech or the interview. He wants to spread the word.' But Terry was getting exhausted. Sure he wanted to spread the word but more and more he started to worry about the run. Was he going to be able to finish? Was he going to have to stop? Was he making enough miles to stay ahead of the winter? He could feel the old health draining away like the gas going out of the tank. He'd lie down on the bed in the motel room and they'd all say 'But Terry we promised you'd come and talk. There's all these people waiting to hear your voice.' That pillow must have felt so soft and so warm. Well, he'd lie there and stare at the ceiling and then he'd get up and get in the van. He must have wondered just who it was that owned Terry Fox."

A highway carved through the rock.
Blackflies as big as hummingbirds.
A menu with every kind of fish you could want.

"Some people are meteors flashing at night across the sky."
"They leave some light glowing behind in the darkest night."

Total defeat or total victory - what the oracle foretold - battered and bruised stump - whispering his dreams - a map of canada - ignore the state of my health - nothing more painful - good luck swallowing bad luck - look into the future.

There's the physical and there's the mental.
Hares lose. Turtles win. The biggest difference has to be the shell.
People tried to draw me out. Why are you doing this to yourself? I pulled my head back in like a turtle and lived inside.

"Invest only in what you love," the wise investor told his son.
"It's the best investment advice that I can give."

Running between South River and Trout Creek.
A person rummaging around in a bag of screwdrivers.
The artificial limb is giving me trouble. I've had trouble all along. Everybody I talk to says the same. – These devices are not made for what you're doing. – They're not made for running a marathon a day. Well, someday maybe they will be. Maybe someday I could work with a designer. Design an artificial leg that can stand up to a human. I could take each one and test it. Give it a test like it wouldn't believe. Bring it up to the standard that I always set for myself. Better springs, better harness, better cup. All these things to do when I finish the

run.

"Evidence of this can be seen along the continental margins of interior British Columbia and in Newfoundland, where the edge of the Canadian Shield is thin and faulted and covered with shallow-marine sedimentary rocks."

Running for the sake of running?
Running for a single ideal?
With only a marathon as the sufficient thought for the day?

"Phidippides was running. From Marathon to Athens. A shorter run this time, but brutal in the sunshine. He was pounding out the miles. He staggered at times and faltered. He clutched at the pain in his side. He lost his way at times. Dizzy; disoriented. His water bottle empty; forgot to fill it at the spring. How could such a thing be happening? What if I take the wrong trail? I have run this way many times. I have run all over the landscape. General to general; battle to battle; city to city and back again. Why so difficult now? Athens is waiting; I bring the message; I cannot fail."

Mobert - Hemlo - Pringle - Marathon - Neys - Jackfish - Terrace Bay - Shrieber - Rossport - Pays Plat - Nipigon - Hurket - Quimet - Pearl - [Terry Fox Memorial] - Thunder Bay - Rosslyn - Kakabeca Falls - Mokomon - Kaministiquia - Finmark - Shabaqua Corners - Raith - Upsala - English River - Ignace - Borups Corners - Dinowic - Wabigoon - Dryden - Oxdrift - Minnitaki - Vermillion Bay - Willard Lake - Longbow Lake - Kenora - Clearwater Bay.

"At Blind River, Terry Fox will be able to record two thousand, seven hundred and thirty-four miles as his total on his quest to reach the Pacific Ocean before the winter sets in."

"Remember that summer when I ran clear across Canada? It's almost thirty years ago now. Who would have thought that the years would go by so fast?"

Running between Sturgeon Falls and Yellek.
A person bending over in terrible pain.
Ankle starting to hurt again. Cough is getting worse. Triggers a pain down deep in my chest. Every time I cough I get that pain. I don't know what it is. Everything else is fine – legs, arms, head. These doctors want me to take a rest, but as long as people keep coming out to see me I'll keep on going. The crowds are thin but they're with me all the way. Put it all out of my mind. My mantra is "a marathon a day".

"Terry speaks with confidence and passion of the mission that he is on. Whatever the difficulties and doubts which he encountered in the early days of the run have clearly dissipated. No doubt, as he approaches the half-way mark in his run across the entire length of Canada, Terry is confident that he will reach his goal."

"No other runner has ever done this."
"Terry Fox is one of a kind."

A person celebrating his fiftieth birthday.
Sleeping by the roadside when we're too far from a motel.
Hearing screams in the cancer ward night after night.

"There were a couple of dozen of us standing around outside. The word had gotten around that he was inside. I was just visiting my cousin and we were out for a walk. Terry was resting inside and the lady was doing his laundry. There'd been so much media and crowds that he needed a place to rest. We were curious, so we went over to the house. Nothing to see. Just a house in a quiet neighbourhood. Everybody was polite. A lot of whispering. I heard all about his story while I was there. About the cancer, and the walk and the raising of funds for cancer research. Just once, the lady came out and shushed us. Told us Terry was sound asleep. We were all pretty embarrassed. Didn't want to wake him up. So my cousin and I thought we'd better leave him alone. Must be difficult being so famous. Having to sneak away and hide to get some rest."

A waterfall tumbling down a rock-face.
A logging road leading off into the bush.
Snowshoes hanging on a restaurant wall.

The audacity of it all - to side-step life - the pain that i see every day - something that's bigger than you - torturous weather and road conditions - trying to find something - falling down inside a dark well - nothing more dead-serious - see you again sometime - the impossible can be done.

I tried to separate myself from everything that I thought would hold me back. I had to put everything into the run. I had to withdraw from people in order to survive.

Rika wanted to come on the run but I told her no. She used to come to the house and type my essays and time me when I went out on those practice-runs. It was a relationship that I had to leave behind.

Even Doug and I had our problems. He was like a brother to me. Some brothers get along great and some not so well.

"You must concentrate your focus," said the guru.
"I will do so," said the acolyte in return.

Running, running, running. Between Beaucage and Meadowville. Getting closer and closer to the half-way mark. Can't wait to put my foot on that half-way spot.

A person reading by the overhead light in a van.

Stopping beside the van. Been fuming all the time I've been running along. Ripping into Darrell. Terry has it easy? – All he has to do is run? Is that what you told them? It's on the front page! What did you tell them that for? Darrell is Cinderella? – Getting Terry's drinks? – Preparing Terry's food? – Sweeping out the van? – Putting up with Terry's rants! You're going to ruin the whole campaign if you keep talking like this to the newspapers! Have you forgotten why we're doing this? We need the money for cancer research! If you keep talking this way, we won't get another dime! So what if you said you don't mind – I know what he's going through – He's running all day! That's the part they leave out! The media's starting to find us boring! They're looking for dirt to spice it up! And you were stupid enough to fall right into their lap! Well, from now on, you're going to be silent! From now on, Darrell Fox does not talk to the press! Do you hear me! From now on, you just leave all the talking to me!

"Terry Fox was serenaded in the rain today as well-wishers lined the route to wish the one-legged marathon runner a happy twenty-second birthday. The special event comes as Terry approaches the half-way mark in his run across Canada in support of cancer research. There are plans for a special cake and a chow-down of Terry's favourite meal of hamburgers and french fries."

Instructing the guys to never break my concentration.
Refusing to turn up for another medical.

Giving a talk about cancer at a fire hall.
A runner bringing news to the folks at home.
Splashing and laughing in the lake after running my miles.

"The fame was all behind him now as far as he was concerned. Kicking the football for sixteen thousand fans. Throwing out the baseball to start the televised game. Listening to ten thousand people chanting 'Terry! Terry! Terry!' at City Hall. It wasn't hard for him to turn his back. He needed it for the fund-raising but he didn't need it for himself. I think he felt that from now on the fame was going to take care of itself. No more phoning ahead at night when he was exhausted and asking an organizer if he could scare up a small crowd and a tiny donation. No more asking the local TV stations and the newspapers to give him a few lines on the evening telecast or a few sentences in the corner of the newspaper. Now what he needed was the run. Just the road and the valleys and the hills. Just the sky and the fields and the trees. He knew he only had so much energy. He knew that the fame was taking its toll. He needed to get away from the fame and get on with the run."

A rowboat knocking gently against a dock.
A backyard barbecue with everyone in town.
A woman whacking a rug on a clothesline.

"His journey is silent – known only to him."
"Only Terry Fox could know what he has endured."

Extremely challenging landscape - left everything behind - deliver the message - concentrate on everything - mountain had not moved - running in a media glow - athens is saved - a man building a house - your victory over me - could only do so much.

I didn't feel that it was unfair. That's the thing about cancer – I wasn't the only one. It happens all the time to all kinds of people.

I learned to joke about it in the classrooms. I showed the kids my mechanical leg. I told them I only wore out half as many socks.

My hair wasn't curly until I got cancer. The curly hair improved my looks. People smiled when I told them that cancer was good to me.

A messenger came to a runner in a dream.
"The gods have held a meeting.
Some of the gods were on your side and some were not."

Running between Wahnipitae and Coniston. I want to stop and celebrate when we reach exactly half-way.

A reporter making notes as a doctor speaks.

Taking inventory again. Nine miles on the new leg today. My stump is raw and bleeding. Took a shower and the hot water scalded my skin. Put the old leg on and ran the rest of the miles. Reporters saw the blood. They phoned the War Amps in Ottawa. Now it's all in the news. There's even odds about whether I'll make it. Urging me to see a doctor. Well, I've got news for them. No doctor in the world has had a patient with an artificial leg who's running a marathon a day for five thousand miles. I'm not going to see any doctors. I don't care what the doctors say. I'm going to keep running until I'm done.

Sharp rocks; desert sands.
Why did you choose such a path?

The whole family around the table at our feast.
Nursing a swollen ankle for mile after mile.
Wearing the sole off another running shoe.

A mile at a time.
Day after day.

"Off what is now eastern North America an ocean developed that probably rivalled the modern Atlantic Ocean in size, but it did not last long."

Birds sing at sunrise.
Always have; always will.

Are you finding things inside that you weren't aware of?
A little better Terry Fox and a little worse?
Discovering things about yourself as you eat up the miles?

Near Sudbury. A picnic table alongside the road. Doug and Darrell stay in the van while I eat alone.
A half-eaten plate of french fries in a garbage pail.
How could the two of them let this happen! Doug just had the van checked and the odometer isn't right! Why do we find out now! So I already passed half-way and I didn't know? Ran right past it as if I was blind? I wanted to stop and savour the moment! Wanted to stop and get my breath and take a nice cold slug of water and look around! Wanted to look down the highway east and then look west! Would have been exactly half-way across Canada and on my way home! And now that moment has been buried under thousands of others! Why didn't they think to check the odometer? It's the memory that I want! This is too damn hard to let it go by in a blur!

Chapter 12

Running in Northern Ontario. Nothing but me and the rocks and the trees. I don't allow myself to think about Rika. She'll be there when I get back to BC.

Two young people dressed up for a high school dance.

You have to keep your distance from people. Like the media people and the doctors and the War Amps representatives. Now they're asking why don't I give it up and just do the cancer promotion from now on. – You've done your best, Terry. – You've made your point and there's nothing left to prove. – You're only going to damage your health if you keep on running. I love the people who cheer me on and I like to talk with them when I can, but that little girl who cried when she saw the blood on my shorts didn't realize that there's something at stake here that's bigger than a few drops of blood. I'll only stop this run if the run stops me.

I will never give up – I will always do my best.

The second-largest country in the world.
Valleys, fishing villages, rocks and trees.
Getting the guys out of bed to talk when I just can't sleep.

Either I'm going to make it or I'm not going to make it.

"By the end of Cambrian time, about 500 million years ago, a process called subduction began. This is the same process that is occurring around the edge of most of the present Pacific Ocean and is responsible for most of the world's most violent earthquakes."

People can live with cancer and die with cancer and still be winners.

What is a boy with family and friends?
What is a boy with sports and a car?
What is a boy shooting baskets and running the track?

Running between Whitefish and Nairn Centre. Thinking about my family. I think about my family all the time.

A crumpled-up newspaper lying on the floor.

There's nothing more painful than reading about yourself. There's no one in the world who can write accurately about what you are. Your own parents couldn't tell your story. I had to stop Darrell from talking to the media, and he's my own brother. Even my diary is just the facts. It won't be able to tell the whole story if anybody ever reads it. There's truth and there's truth and there's truth. It's hard enough to tell the truth yourself without others telling it for you. These writers are all just looking for an angle. An angle and the truth are not the same.

"There are reports of tension in the camp of Terry Fox, who is running across Canada in support of funds for cancer research. It is said that his handlers want to maximize the number of speaking engagements and receptions in order to take advantage of Terry's popularity, while Terry wants to limit himself to one speaking engagement a day in order to concentrate on the run itself."

"Hear the stump is giving him trouble."
"Hear he's got a persistent cough."

"Chemotherapy is a drug treatment which uses powerful chemicals to kill fast-growing cells in your body. Chemotherapy is often used to treat cancer, since cancer cells grow and multiply much more quickly than most cells in the body. Many different chemotherapy drugs are available. Chemotherapy drugs can be used alone or in combination to treat a wide variety of cancers. Though chemotherapy is an effective way to treat many types of cancer, it also carries a risk of side effects. Some chemotherapy side effects are mild and treatable, while others can cause serious complications."

"It's the myth of the hero. We were talking about it in my classroom. Every society has had a similar story. How a young boy rises up out of the midst. A boy of humble origins. Perhaps he'll have a handicap. Perhaps his size, or a speech impediment, or in this case, a missing leg. And he will rise up and perform a heroic deed. He will find his role in society. He will make a contribution. An act that will save many lives or define a culture. He summons up all his assets, using talents that no one suspects that he has, to perform some great, heroic feat of epic proportions. And his culture recognizes him. They thank him for the benefits. They grant him the accolades. And then he takes his humble place in society again. All of these cultural myths are similar. All of them differ slightly somehow. There are variations on what happens after the deed is done."

Trucks gearing down to take a hill.
An old fellow waxing a pair of skis.
A barn with a sign that says there's antiques inside.

The thing that pulls me down - the giant didn't notice - oldest rocks on earth - fragments of the failure - taking canada into my eyes - release from the runner's toil - thinking about cancer - a topic we didn't touch - another celebrity.

I settled into a routine. The van went ahead one mile exactly. I ran to the van, got a drink or shook my head, and then the van pulled ahead for exactly another mile.

There was always blood on my shorts. Blood in the cup of my artificial leg. The drops of blood were the price I had to pay.

Hill after hill and valley after valley. The humidity and the heat. I absorbed Canada into my bloodstream mile after mile.

"Well if your feet have lotsa rock," the grandfather said,
"You'll always know that your feet are on the ground."

Running Between Espanola and Webwood. There's a prison up ahead. They've got me scheduled to give a talk.

A prisoner looking out through the bars of a jail.

So what do I say? That I know what it's like to be in prison? Every one of them will probably laugh. But I've been in prison before. What's a cancer ward if not a prison? Think of those kids in the cancer ward. They lie awake and scream. I've heard screams that would blister your ears. You'll all be out when you've served your time. Those kids get out when they're sent to the morgue. A cancer ward is a prison without any hope.

"The organization which has provided and maintained the artificial leg that Terry Fox is using in his run for cancer has responded to reports of blood being visible on Terry's shorts by saying that he is going to run into terrific problems with his stump if he does not take time off to heal the wounds which are being inflicted by his relentless campaign to run across Canada before the winter sets in."

Cringing at a last-minute invitation to a village fair.

Telling a crowd that I could easily get cancer again.

Peeling off my bloody sock after every run.
A story-teller getting ready to tell a story.
Rika and I writing letters that ask for support.

"Things began to get more intense near the end. Don't forget it was twenty-six miles a day. The pain was getting worse – the body was breaking down – winter was coming on – the end of September. He wanted to focus on the run. Once he got the day's run done he could relax. But if you talked to him along the run, he could be a little surly. He didn't like to have to stop and talk to the crowds. He'd rather run right through their town and then drive back in the evening and relax and talk. Get himself dry – get some clean clothes – know that he'd done his work that day – another day, another marathon in the books. That's why some people found him snappy and a little abrupt. He'd be standing there in the cold and covered in sweat, knowing there was half or more of the miles still to run. And he was expected to be charming and cheerful and give everybody lots of his time. The people who saw the charming Terry – friendly and chatty and completely at ease – they're the ones who saw him after his daily run."

Water rushing fiercely in a stream.
A boy with a big grin and a mess of trout.
A lake with water as clear as a pane of glass.

"He runs in the darkness when we're all asleep."
"When the sun comes up he's already far into his run."

Invade surrounding tissue - there was another terry - heat and cold and misery - machine that renews itself - only reason we're here - keep the vision pure - a little girl who lost her hair - just had to tell - if i have to crawl - question the enormous burden.

The reporters will build you up. The reporters will tear you down. What kind of story are we going to write today?

Let's make the kid look good. Let's make the kid look bad. Good or bad, bad or good, as long as it sells.

I think the lowest part was when that reporter wrote that I didn't run through Quebec. Him sitting and writing in his air-conditioned office and me out here on the highway running on blistering pavement for mile after mile. How could anybody write that kind of thing?

Son of my father; father of my son, thought the investor.
Which investments will provide the highest yields?

Running between Spanish and Algoma Mills. Darrell's giving me the silent treatment. I'm giving him the same.

Two young men smiling faintly for the camera.

I know the media's just a game. Something every day to perk up the ears. First it's a kid on one leg who's trying to run. Then it's the kid making some progress – let's cheer him on. Then it gets a little dull. Mile after mile after mile – all the same. Then somebody sees some blood on his shorts. Hey! We can make something out of this! Let's ask all kinds of doctors what are the odds? Make it a guessing game for the readers. How many think the kid is going to fail? But the reporters don't know pain. And the doctors don't know pain. I've seen people in pain and this is nothing. They want to know about pain? The reporters think the story is me, but it's not. It's the kids in the cancer wards. Let them go and lie in a cancer ward in the middle of the night. Let them lie there and listen to the screams and keep asking themselves, hour by hour, what they can do about it. People who want me to quit running are people who don't want to face the pain. I faced the pain in the cancer ward every night.

"During subduction, oceanic crust bends down and is swallowed up beneath the continental margin, and the tectonic processes that result include the building of mountain belts and chains of volcanoes, resulting in much disruption of the local geology."

What is a boy who runs smack into cancer?
What is a boy who loses his leg?
What is a boy who listens to children screaming in pain?

"The run to Athens was brutal. Phidippides coughed up blood. A shorter run than to Sparta, but much more taxing by far. At times he wondered if he would make it. Blood was seeping through his tunic; the wound that he hid from his general as he answered the call. He would never have let me run. No other should carry this news. It is I who have made a commitment. I who spoke with the green-god Pan. He has given us the victory. He has been true in his word to Athens; he will be true in his word to me. He made a promise that I am counting on; I made a promise too. To give all that I have to this race that I must run."

Whiteshell - Faloma - Falcon Lake - East Braintree - Prada - Rocher - Paradise Village - Deacon's Corner - Winnipeg - Headley - Cartier - Elie - Portage la Prairie - Macgregor - Austin - Sidney - Douglas - Brandon - Kemnay - Alexander - Oak Lake - Virden - Hargrove - Kirkella - Fleming - Moosomin - Wapella - Whitewood - Percival - Broadview - Oakshela - Grenfell - Wolseley - Sintaluta - Indian Head - Qu'Appelle - McLean - Balsome - Emerald Park - Regina.

"Sault Ste. Marie brings Terry Fox to the two thousand, nine hundred mile marker as he continues his triumphant journey across the face of Canada in pursuit of the eradication of the scourge of cancer."

"I was only eighteen when I lost my leg to cancer. Losing my leg was pretty traumatic. But the amputation was the thing that gave me such a long life."

Running through Blind River and Iron Bridge. Reading the newspapers at every stop. Watching TV.
A tourist admiring the scenery from a railway dome.
Warnings from the War Amps office in Ottawa. Giving interviews to reporters from their desks. Predicting the problems I'll have with the stress on my stump. – His stump will be changing shape. – He'll develop open sores. – He'll suffer restricted blood-flow. – He should stop and take a rest and get proper care. Well I've got news for the experts. For the reporters and everyone else. I was alone on the highway in Newfoundland. Blood was running down my leg. All the experts would have said give it up and go home. If I'd wanted an easy ride – from the Atlantic to the Pacific – I could have bought a ticket and looked at the scenery all the way across Canada. And how much money would have come in while I sat on the train?

"The Cancer Society representative who has been travelling with Terry Fox has reportedly left the run and neither Terry Fox nor the two remaining members of the entourage – Terry's brother Darrell and his driver, Doug – will comment on rumours that a rift has developed in which the representative is having trouble balancing the requests of his Cancer Society superiors with Terry Fox's ideas as to what is best for himself and for his run."

"Hear he hasn't been taking those x-rays."
"Probably doesn't want to know what they'll say."

Hearing every word people shout as I'm running along.
A bag of balloons rising up and floating away.
Driving myself to exhaustion day after day.

"I've seen Terry when he was up and when he was down. It wasn't just a case of running up those hills and running down into those valleys along the way. It was a case of living on the raw edge of what it was to be alive. Here was a kid on only one leg, blood dripping into his shorts with every mile, pain that most of us wouldn't stand for without a battery of doctors feeding us pain-killers, and running – every day – what knocks a marathon-runner out for at least a week. Then as soon as he got famous, he became the poster-boy for cancer, and was in demand for a big rally in every little town he passed through along the way. People who sat at a desk all day, or worked a lathe at a factory, would listen to him speak and give their dollars and say 'Keep up the good work, Terry' and then go to their kid's baseball game and relax in the bleachers and then go home and watch a little TV. And here was Terry, tumbling into bed, after a day that would knock out a plough horse, and getting up next morning at four-thirty on the dot and running a marathon. He was living at the basic core of life every day."

Pickup trucks with deer across the fenders.
A group of kids lined up outside a movie theatre.
A hitchhiker with a knapsack on his back.

Know no agony - the kids were living in pain - second half of my life - needing replacement parts - whatever just broke - the deeper motive - both were terry fox - the force of gravity - living in the present - tougher days ahead.

My mom and dad flew down to Nova Scotia. I was crying over the phone. They came right away to help me deal with Doug.

When my brother, Darrell, joined me in New Brunswick, I felt so relieved. It was like having my mom and dad and my brothers and sister along on the run. Doug was a friend, of course he was, but there's something about family that nothing else can replace.

I just stood there and hugged with Darrell. A great day when he arrived. He came the day he finished his high school exams.

"But on what shall I focus my attention?" asked the acolyte.
"You must concentrate your focus on everything," the guru replied.

Running through Iron Bridge. This has been pretty rough on Doug. He gets snarly sometimes but he never threatens to quit.
Two people eating silently at a picnic table.
I was free to walk away. When the x-rays cleared me of cancer, I was free to walk away and leave it behind. But I couldn't go on with my life. I'd see the faces contorted in pain. I'd hear the screams in the night when they thought there was no one to help. I just couldn't walk away. I live with the faces and the screams. That's why I drive myself so hard. I drive myself to exhaustion so I can sleep at night.

"A reporter in Terry Fox's home province of British Columbia has written an article in which he questions whether Terry actually ran through the province of Quebec. A spokesman for Terry has countered by claiming not only that he ran every mile, but that there are hundreds of witnesses at various stages along the route who would gladly refute such potentially-damaging charges."

Giving a speech about Doug and feeling better.
Running in the lightning and the rain.

A pygmy in the presence of a giant.
Talking to people after all the cameras are gone.
Bill sitting and waiting for word on those hotel stairs.

"The birthday party was really something. We didn't know what was gonna happen but we knew it was going to be interesting. We had a cake made up for Terry. And we were going to present it to him, but we couldn't be sure of his mood. So anyways, Terry looks all solemn and serious. It had been raining all day. People in plastic garbage bags and a fairly difficult run, so maybe he wasn't in the mood for any hijinks. So Terry takes it from Darrell, still with a serious face, reads the writing on the cake and then tries to flip it in Darrell's face. So there's this scuffle outside the restaurant. Then the reporters took their pictures. Terry and Darrell and Doug and Bill all covered with the icing from Terry's cake! A toilet seat around Terry's shoulders and a silly grin on his face! Every one of us had a good laugh. Then we all went in and ate. The restaurant had another cake, so we all chowed-down with cake and cherry coke."

Fishing gear stowed in a canoe.
Bags of ice for sale beside a store.
A driver backing a truck into a loading dock.

"He knows every blade of grass from here to Newfoundland."
"He's left a footprint on every inch of ground in between."

Hollowed out at the end - nightmare in brutal sunlight - exhausted and in pain - how to keep things separate - entirely out of your control - hand-to-hand combat - find out what you're made of inside - a slow-moving ceiling fan - a backyard barbecue - what has transpired.

It's the luck of when you were born. Ten years ago, I probably would have died. By funding cancer research, we can speed up time.

Everything I do is for cancer research. I'm doing something that nobody else has done. No more kids screaming in pain in the cancer wards.

It never occurred to me that I would ever get cancer again. As far as I was concerned, for me, cancer was a thing of my past. It was other people who were suffering – the people who were screaming in the cancer wards, day after day, night after night – that I was running for.

"The meeting lasted for hours.

There were many speeches made.
I have some bad news and some good news to relate."

Running, running, running. No way I'm going to get that cancer-check.
A sleeper with eyeballs flickering under the lids.

I've only had one dream while I've been running. Most nights, I'm too exhausted to do anything but sleep. Maybe I've had lots of them. How would I know? Just once I woke up and glanced at the clock. A little after midnight. And the dream was there for me. Like a picture on a screen. There was an empty balcony railing. And then this cat jumps up on top. And then it walks along the railing. And there's noises of horns honking and traffic down below. And then suddenly someone opens the apartment door.

Narrow pathway; steep climb.
What is there to gain?

Heat, humidity, lack of sleep.
A person deciding that a mountain will never move.
Putting the bad days behind me, one at a time.

Forging ahead.
Mind on the goal.

"The oceanic crust that undergoes subduction is reabsorbed into the mantle. Geological evidence indicates that the island of Newfoundland contains remnants of the destruction by subduction of an entire ocean."

Birds nest at sunset.
Always have; always will.

What is a man with pain in his heart?
What is a man with fire in his eyes?
What is a man who runs on one leg over thousands of miles?

Running through Thessalon and Bruce Mines. Someday I'll dip my foot in the ocean and smile.
A runner with a frown on his brow looking straight ahead.
A truck pulls up beside the van. A guy rolls down his window and says he's a welder. He was watching TV at his house and the announcer said that I was having trouble with my artificial leg. So he jumped in his truck and drove along the highway looking for our van. Says he'd like to have a look at the leg and see if there's anything he can do. Chatting with the welder as he does a job on the prosthetic leg. Welding mask and a three-day beard. A friendly, talkative

fellow. Turning my eyes away each time he makes a weld. Three kids? So what are their ages? Oh really? Do they like to play games? Do you have a backyard? Got a dog or any other pets? So what do you and your wife and your kids all do for fun? He chuckles as he talks. The only question that I don't ask him – Is every one of your kids in the best of health?

Chapter 13

Running, running, running. Running from Desbarat to Echo Bay. People cheering me as I run. A dizzy spell but I keep on running. A shake or two to clear my head.

A one-legged runner posing for pictures with a group of kids.

Nice to be in the routine. Twenty-six miles every day. Lots of water, lots of rock, lots of trees. Small crowds along the way. Stop and talk for a moment or two, but I don't want to lose my pace. The guys from the van collect with their buckets. Always grateful for every cent. Some people tell me I should smile more, but I'm not doing this for fun. Hope the crowds know I'm glad to be here, even though there's a scowl on my face. Together, we can lick this thing. That's the one thing I know for sure. It's when we don't all pull together that things go wrong.

I'm not going to quit and let everyone down.

A girl whose mom never recovered from the loss.
Cars with boats and trailers and camping gear buzzing along.
A person leaving a cancer ward for a day.

I'll either make it or be in a hospital bed or be dead.

"The Avalon Peninsula, in the east, represents a sliver of a continent that formerly lay somewhere between Britain and Africa."

I want to set an example that will never be forgotten.

Did you realize that Canada was so vast?
So many miles and so many people from sea to sea?
Wish you were born in a country like Monaco or Lichtenstein?

Running along and thinking. The only place I let myself think. On the road my thoughts are always clear and cold.

A grinning teenager posing with a beat-up old car.

Before my cancer I was very self-centred. I had my sports, my family, my friends, my car and not much else. Being self-centred is not the way I want to live. I couldn't be just a dreamer. I couldn't sit at home and let life go by. I knew that I would have to get out and run. I ran for sixteen months to get ready to run across Canada. I was toughening up my leg – of course I was. I was toughening up my lungs and my heart the way a marathon runner does. But there was something else I was doing. I was toughening up my mind. I knew I'd need twice the mind to run on half the legs. So I will not give up this run. I will not give up this run. I will die before I will ever give up this run.

"Calls for Terry Fox to take a break from his gruelling schedule have been met with uncharacteristic scorn from Terry, who is usually so easy-going with the press. His usual charm was missing today as Terry told a group of reporters that he refuses to listen to those who he feels are – no matter how public-spirited – threatening to undermine his efforts at a successful run."

"Doesn't matter to him what's the weather."
"He's running through rain and storm."

"Cancer and its treatment can cause several complications including pain, fatigue, difficulty breathing, nausea, diarrhea or constipation, weight loss, chemical changes in your body, brain and nervous system problems, unusual immune system reactions to cancer, cancer that spreads to other parts of the body, and cancer that returns."

"Near the end he got down to the core. The noise and the clutter faded away. He was reducing himself to his essence. Finding the level at which things were pure. Willing himself to run with no more fuel than desire. The aches and the pains were still inside him, but they were an asset, like a pearl. Nothing got in the way of the running. There was just water and rock and trees. Just a boy running for miles with his eyes on the road."

A tiny island with a cottage perched on the rock.
A bathtub filled with flowers in front of a house.
Kids with pool cues out on the sidewalk taking a look.

A mental question - scrabble a few people together - yesterday's water - empty dark room - staying in the groove - taken over by a force - to give something back - writing in my journal - heal the wound - returned to the oracle.

I set myself a thousand goals. To that sign-post up ahead; to that driveway where the car is backing out; to that tree with the crooked branch hanging over the road. I set myself a thousand goals a day.

I chanted as I ran. Cancer - pain - death. Money - research - life. Children sick - children treated - children cured.

"And, if your boat has lotsa water," the grandfather added,
"You'll always be able to go where the big ones go."

Running through Garden River. Everybody clapping and calling my name. A half-a dozen school kids keeping pace with me. This has to be just about perfect. Wonderful weather.

A young girl with an autograph book and a beaming smile.

What a beautiful little town. Seems like everybody's come out to see me. Everybody smiling and waving hello. Everybody's carrying a sign. – Welcome to Garden River, Terry! Just seems too good to be true. On the home stretch and running through every little town along the way. And the pain is just a small hurdle that I can jump over. It all seems too good to be true. – Too good to be true. – Too good to be true. – Too good to be true.

"The disclosure that Terry Fox has avoided almost all of the scheduled medical checkups on his way across Canada has caused a number of people to wonder whether there is a reason why Terry – despite the wishes of the Cancer Society, the War Amps and many medical observers – is refusing all efforts at providing medical help."

Wondering what I can do about my cysts.
Running behind the van to cut the wind.

Blisters, open sores, blood in the bucket.
Taking Darrell aside and telling him what I'm thinking.
A backyard barbecue with everybody having a great time.

"It was near the end that it all seemed to change for Terry. It became harder for him to take his part in the fun. For the rest of us, it could have gone on just the same. Have Terry's water ready, keep track of every mile, have a dry sock handy for when he needs a change. Don't talk to him while he's running. Let him concentrate on the task. Be ready for hijinks in the evenings. Whatever

Terry might need to lighten his mood. Or leave him alone in his room with the light off so he can ease himself past the latest storm of pain. We could have gone on like that forever – we were safely in a groove. But all the things that Terry needed to keep on running – stamina, health, manageable pain – all of these things that had kept him going for so long – just seemed as if they were slowly slipping away."

Crowds of people gathered at a cross-roads.
A stand selling bakers' dozens of fresh sweet corn.
A family in the glow of a crackling fire.

"He has amazing reserves of endurance."
"He is overcoming hurdles that would break anyone else."

Assembled from continental fragments - wound in his side - sources of light - too good to be true - more important than me - two people riding silently - turn against myself - how the story has gone so far - feel like a phony - aware of everything.

I know what the doctors know. They know I need some rest. What they don't know is why I won't take their advice.

I know that my stump is changing shape. I know that I'm developing a lot more sores. I don't need a doctor to tell me what I already know.

It's not a mental question for me. The only question is physical. If I don't make it, it will be because my body has let me down.

He invested in the air which we breathe.
He invested in the fire by which we stay warm.

Trucks roaring by on the highway. Glancing at a newspaper while I take a break. Feeling sick to my stomach! How could they write this kind of thing! *A small crowd surrounding a runner on his water-break.* Saying I didn't run through Quebec! That I rode all the way in the van! This reporter is out in Vancouver! Thousands of miles away from my run! Why wouldn't he tell the truth! If he knew how tired I'm getting! How I've always told the truth! How I've ground out every mile! How important it is that I never miss a foot! He could have flown out here and run with me, but instead he thinks up stories instead of the news! Doug says he'll phone and get a retraction! There's thousands of witnesses along the route! That'll be nice – that'll be nice – but it won't replace whatever just broke inside of me! You work so hard to build something up, and then you look around for a moment, and there's someone who's working hard at tearing it down!

"In Gros-Morne National Park it is possible to see where a fragment of the Earth's oceanic crust and mantle was pushed up over the ancient continental margin during the subduction process."

Why is there always blood on your shorts?
Why is there never relief from the pain?
Why do you put off meeting a doctor mile after mile?

"Phidippides was running. He fought for the future; he fought through his pain. I have served my city faithfully; run the messages; carried the word. Heat and cold and misery; hunger and thirst and an aging knee. But now I shall live at home. At one with my parents, at one with my clan. Huts in a circle; sharing the fire. I shall marry a certain maiden. I shall have children and sit in the shade. Grow crops and reap the harvest. No more travelling far and wide in the runner's trade. The green-god Pan has promised. 'And as for you Phidippides, I have taken note of you. You are a person who toils for no reward. Give all that you have to this race that you must run. To you I will grant release from the runner's toil.' "

Harbour Landing - Pense - Belle Plaine - Moose Jaw - Caron Caronport - Chaplin - Uren - Emfold - Morse - Herbert - Rush Lake - Waldeck - Swift Current - Beverley - Gull Lake - Carmichael - Tompkins - Piapot - Walsh - Irvine - Dunmore - Medicine Hat - Redcliff - Suffield - Alderson - Tilley - Brooks - Bassano - Cluny - Gleichen - Stathmore - Chestermore - Calgary - Jumping Pond - Seebe - Kanaskis - Dead Man's Flat - Canmore.

"Near Terrace Bay, in Northern Ontario, Terry Fox will reach mile three thousand, two hundred and fifty-five of his epic journey."

"Not everyone was so lucky. There were a lot of young kids in the cancer ward. An awful lot of them were not so lucky as me."

Running between Heyden and Galois River. Splashing through the puddles from yesterday's rain.
An amputee wiping his artificial leg with a motel towel.
The War Amps don't know what they're doing. They're undermining the cause. Sure my stump is changing shape. Sure my stump is covered with sores. Sure there's blood in the valve of my artificial leg. But don't ask me to slow down the pace. Don't ask me to take a rest. Don't ask me to see any specialists. I know what they're going to say. Sure the War Amps mean to help. They don't like to see me in pain. What they can't see is the pain that I see every day. I'm not running for myself. If I die from this – so what? I'm doing this for those kids in the cancer wards.

"Terry Fox voiced an impassioned plea today, at a stop along the high-way on his route through Northern Ontario, to be allowed to continue his run without a constant barrage of charges that he is damaging his health by not tak-ing time off to rest. He had tears in his eyes as he spoke of the young cancer victims who cannot take a day off from the pain in which they are living and insisted that what little pain he is undergoing is nothing compared to what some of those young cancer victims are suffering through."

"Twenty-six miles, day in day out."
"Be home in BC before the winter sets in."

Rubbing salve on the sores on my leg.
A person sharing a brain with a Siamese twin.
Waiting in Montreal for Canada Day.

"Terry heard every word they shouted. Even if he didn't respond. His face was always grim when he was running. That was the only face he could manage to counter the pain. Near the end they were shouting 'Way to go Terry!' 'You can make it!' 'Don't give up!" and things like that. He knew what they were offering him – and he was soaking it in. He had those terrible pains in his chest but his arms and legs were okay. He'd stop for a while and have a drink or catch his breath and then he'd be at it again. Near the end he'd take breaks in the run. He'd run five or six miles at a stretch, then he'd lie down in the van and wait for the pain in his chest to ease and then he'd go back out to the marker and con-tinue the run. It was the cheers that kept him going. People were lined up along the highway calling out that they were with him. He had to concentrate to run. Sometimes he'd give a little wave and sometimes he wouldn't respond to a shout but those people should know that Terry heard every word."

A train whistle sounding in the night.
A cup of coffee on a dock first thing in the morning.
A deer upside down dripping blood.

The best thing that you've got - children smiling for the camera - as close as i can get - tear it all to shreds - a super-human effort - more than they have to give - drifting through life - more than just photographs - to lose with grace - i might get caught.

I was helped by a lot of people along the way. I had never given speech-es. I had never organized a cancer run.

That young teacher was really great. She sat with me in the stairwell. She told me how to relax and talk to the kids.

Bill was a superb cancer organizer. He slept all night in his car. He got up even earlier than me on his very first day.

"Every garden is a desert; every desert is a garden.
Every grain of sand is a mountain; every mountain a grain of sand."

Running through Agawa Bay. There's something funny going on! The crowds are great but they're making me nervous! Everybody seems to be holding up a sign!
A scowling man amid a crowd of smiling well-wishers.
Stopping and talking to the crowds. So what is this you're saying? Sault Ste. Marie to Thunder Bay? Every town between the two? Wawa? Marathon? Nipigon? Each one claims to be half-way? I keep stopping and explaining! No, you're wrong! Your signs are wrong! I'm more than half-way! Don't tell me these miles don't count! They're being measured in drops of blood! You've got to change your signs! I'm more than half-way!

"A newspaper reporter has apologized today and retracted a story in which he alleged that Terry Fox – due to a disappointing reception in that province – had not run all of the miles in the Quebec leg of his cross-country run for cancer. In an uncharacteristically emotional outburst, Terry Fox said that the false report had broken his heart when he read it and had shaken his faith in the media and the press."

Pouring catsup on my hamburger.
Giving a speech in a high school gym.

Living in the present, not the past.
A handful of diamonds sparkling on the snow.
Writing in my journal on a picnic table.

"I gave him three hundred dollars. Now that's a lot of money. I'm a cleaning lady and it requires a lot of work to make that sum. I was saving it for a bus trip. You take a bus to Atlantic City – you get the bus and you share a room and you get a voucher for a couple of meals and you get to gamble for two nights and two days and then you come home. I counted it out and sent it off to the cancer people in town on behalf of Terry. I've never had cancer myself. I know I'm never going to get it. I know I'll be cleaning people's apartments for a good long time. But the elderly lady I used to clean for died of cancer. She had it for quite a few years – a long slow decline. I used to help her daughter on my day off. Didn't have to do it – they weren't relatives of mine. But the lady was always so cheerful. Used to make me a cup of tea. We'd sit and talk in her kitchen. I insisted that I had work to do but she insisted we sit and talk. She wanted to sit at the dining room table but I insisted that the kitchen was fine. I used to spend the whole day there. The daughter paid me for half a day but I didn't mind. The cancer was eating away inside her as she was telling me about her life. She loosened me up so I was willing to talk about mine. So near the end, when it got so awkward, I'd show up on my day off and help the daughter take her to the clinic for the chemo treatments. She was old, this little old lady, but she always made me smile. And her daughter was pretty sad when she came to die. So when I read about Terry Fox, I just counted out my money – my Atlantic City money – and sent it all to the cancer people in town."

A snowmobile sitting in a yard.
A gentle rocking in the wake of a passing water-skier.
A lady telling a story to her grand-kids.

"He's reaching down deeper inside himself than most can imagine."
"He's kept his promise to every child in the cancer ward."

Proliferation of anaplastic cells - a small group of people - most noticeable aspect - searching for the marker - the best of us - the physical and the mental - this epic journey - drain my hope away - according to promise.

The next time we have Christmas dinner, I'll be able to relax. The last time, all I could think about was the run. Just my family and me and a few others – Rika and Doug.

A cancer ward with no screaming. A cancer ward with no one there. A cancer ward in an empty building and a sign, "For Lease".

Never again – never again – never again. Never again will there be cancer. Never again.

"The gods who voted against you won the day.
In the end, it was decided by a single vote.
They have decided that you will only have one leg."

Trying to clear up something important. Stopping and talking to the crowds.

A young boy proudly holding up a sign.

How can I only be half-way? I know I reached it back near Sudbury! So why do all the signs say I'm only half-way? Everybody smiling and cheering and shouting out that I've finally reached half-way! I keep stopping and telling these people that I'm on the second half! I passed it days ago! I passed it back in Sudbury! You don't seem to understand! You're cheering me, but you're adding extra miles! Please don't tell me I'm only half-way! Please don't tell me I'm falling behind! I know you mean to support me but you're breaking my heart!

This is using up all my time! I'm running for cancer clear across Canada! I don't have time to stop and talk about every sign!

Shortness of breath; constant pain.
Ever tempted to let it go?

The hare and the tortoise in a race.
Waking up beside my artificial leg.
Running up Burrard Mountain day after day.

Stick with the vision.
The end is in sight.

"The belt of deformed rocks which developed during this oceanic closure extends southwestwards through the Atlantic provinces and down the eastern margin of the United States, and is collectively referred to as the Appalachian Orogen."

Know that I won't be here forever.
Can't say that this is wrong.

Suppose they never find a cure for cancer?
Suppose they try but they never reach their goal?
Would that mean that this run has been in vain?

A hotel room near Wawa. Lying on the bed. Lights off and curtains closed.
A pair of shorts, a t-shirt and a single sock on a chair.
I don't want to see any doctors. I know myself better than anyone else. If I went to a doctor every time I got a little cyst or an abrasion, I'd still be back in Nova Scotia. Pain isn't a reason for quitting. I've seen people in a lot more pain. The cancer wards are full of them. My pain is nothing to what they go through. Who's telling them to quit and go home? Sometimes pain is the water you swim in. Sometimes pain is the air you breathe. You can't shut it off every time you feel a little sore. I ran twenty-six miles today. I'm going to run twenty-six miles tomorrow. Not bad for a boy that the experts are trying to write off.

Chapter 14

Running from Hemlo to Pringle. I know I'm slowing down. I have to take more breaks than I used to do.

A tiny figure moving slowly beside a lake.

Running free in Northern Ontario. Lake Superior is gigantic. Running along the north shore. Best scenery a person could ever expect to see. Training my sights on Terrace Bay. Looking beyond to Thunder Bay. Having a good run so far this morning. – Drink of water. – Suck on a lemon. – Washroom break and back on the road. Approaching thirteen miles. Weather perfect. – No wind. – Cool. Almost as if I ordered the weather for today. Talking a bit with the guys. Convinced me to stop at Jackfish Lake. Well, I don't mind taking a break, but just for an hour. The weather's perfect as it is. Let's get the miles in before it changes. You never know what'll happen when you start the day.

I'm not special.

A long highway stretching for miles and miles and miles.
Tracing my finger along a map of Canada.
Trying to remember all those words of high school French.

This just intensifies what I did. It gives it more meaning.

"Its formation took a long time, and was only completed about 250 million years ago, when the tectonic plates corresponding to modern Europe and Africa finally collided with and welded against the eastern North American margin."

It'll inspire more people.

What would you be doing if you had never been touched by cancer?
Riding a camel?, climbing a mountain?, mowing the lawn?
Do you ever imagine a different Terry Fox?

Running, running, running. Marathon ahead. Hills, trees, waterfalls. Rock, sky, road. Thirteen more miles of grinding to make my run for today.
A runner sinking down into the dust.
I don't know a lot about this runner, Phidippides. Somebody mentioned him to me. Back in the days of the Ancient Greeks. He was the first to run a marathon. I looked him up one day in the library. It told a lot about him but I didn't want too many details. Where I wanted to run was a long way from Greece. He ran on two legs, he only ran one race and he died at the end of it. That's about it. I couldn't see that his story had much to say to me. You look at Greece on a map and it isn't very wide. You could probably run across it in a couple of days. Twenty-six miles and then he dropped dead. I'm running twenty-six miles every day.

"As Terry Fox is running behind me here, high up on the Canadian shield, north of Lake Superior, alone amidst the pine forest and the sky, we are told that a Terry Fox frenzy is building in his home province of British Columbia, where, if he maintains his present pace of a marathon a day, Terry is expected to arrive sometime early in December of this year."

"Seems to be finding the north hard going."
"Not as healthy as he was."

"The cure rate for cancer is often tied to its early diagnosis. If you, or anyone you know, has any of the traditional signs of cancer, be sure to see a doctor immediately. Remember that with early detection, proper treatment and supervised recovery, cancer, though fatal in many cases, can sometimes be cured."

"At the end it was almost as if he was in another zone. The one where you stifle the pain so much that it no longer seems like pain. The one where the running is the only thing that exists. All the past has led to this moment. Everything you've been in your life so far. The future holds no interest. It would take you off your task. Just you and your mind and your body and the road."

Miles of burnt-out forest.
A row of bathing suits hanging on a line.
A white sail moving slowly across a lake.

Bitter weather ahead - just a small hurdle - the mental requirements - your stubbornness equals your pain - screams in the cancer ward - to share the pain - a man running alone - a few lines of ink - talked in simple terms - barking like dogs.

I concentrated on running. Running and running and running. I decided that was the best thing I could do.

Keep track of the distances. Keep track of the miles. They're the one thing I could think of that couldn't go bad.

Running across the face of Canada. Asking Canadians to share the pain. Asking everyone to make the pain go away.

"And, if your head has lotsa sky," the grandfather explained,
"You'll always be able to think at the top of your mind."

Running and swimming with Greg Scott. Splashing and shouting in Jackfish Lake.

A baldheaded boy riding a bike with his dad at his side.

Greg's dad brought him to see me. They were waiting in Terrace Bay. Of course I remember Greg! You're from St. Catharines! We met in Hamilton! I didn't forget! Ten years old and a victim of bone cancer. Ten years old and a hairless skull. No more baseball for Greg until he gets his strength back again. Still, he sure can ride that bike. Telling me not to slow down because of him. Keeping me pushing for about six miles. Swimming like a porpoise without his artificial leg. Whooping and hollering in the water. I'll have to get back to swimming. Taking my inspiration from Greg. Pale and skinny and a quiet voice and great big smile of surprise when I remembered his name. Relaxing while towelling off. Having a little talk with Greg's dad. – You came a long way from St. Catharines. – Was it Doug who asked you to bring him? – I've been asking Doug about Greg nearly every day.

"Here in Northern Ontario, Terry Fox today dismissed concerns about the pain that he is in as he continues his Marathon of Hope. He says that reports of bleeding from his stump are exaggerated and that no amount of pain will cause him to abandon his quest to run across Canada by December of this year."

Waving my hand to let them know I hear their shouts.
Correcting speakers who call my run a walk.

A person being eaten by a shark.
A person whose thoughts keep tumbling through his mind.
Rolling out of bed at four A M.

"Near the end Terry started to falter – north of Superior as he ran to-wards Thunder Bay. Perfect weather near the end. It can be so glorious north of Superior – the rock, the trees, the water – light white clouds and sunny blue skies. Open highway for miles ahead. Film crews were buzzing around him. Money was pouring in from all over Canada. The crowds had eased along the roadways so he could talk to them one on one after each day's marathon. Every Canadian was watching and cheering. Fewer of those receptions that were sapping his strength. Everything seemed in place to complete his dream. But it was still an exhausting run – a touch of the flu, sometimes cold rain, inflammation of the tendon, persistent cough, shortness of breath, pain in the chest. All the symptoms of a heart attack. Fear of cancer – but he put it off. Mile after mile after mile – the glorious highway and the fading boy. A nagging fear that soon the run might come to an end."

> *Moose grazing lazily in a field.*
> *A waitress giving the table a quick wipe.*
> *A train snaking along for mile after mile.*

"He's set his sights at the highest level."
"He's achieving what no other human has ever achieved."

The bone-chilling wind - everything seemed in place - every test has shown - a place in your mind - poster-boy for cancer - the cries of the children - an even better chance - kids donating their recess money - strong enough for two.

I'm not a soul in search of myself.
I know who I am and what I'm doing.
I know exactly what I'm doing and I know why.

He invested in the water which we drink.
He invested in the soil in which things grow.

Running, running, running. Media requests at every stop. There's been lots of media coverage since Toronto.

A person watching himself being interviewed on television.

I want positive news reports not negative ones. Why should I pose for their pictures? Why should I answer their questions? Look what they did to Dar-rell. He tells everything about us and then they turn it upside down. You can't even call it news. It's the story of Cinderella with a bunch of new names. You take an old bottle and you pour in Terry Fox and his brother and the van and you've got your story. – The step-sister runs all day, lazing along and enjoying the flowers. – Cinderella sweeps out the van and takes the abuse. So easy to write the story. All you need is some juicy quotes and then you're done. Well, it's positive or nothing. I'm not doing this for myself. If I can't tell who to trust then I won't talk to anyone.

"By this time, much of what is now Eastern Canada and what were then the adjacent areas of Britain and northwest Europe was covered by the world's first large trees in widespread forests that, when buried, turned into coal."

Are there those who get a free ride?
Are there those who know no agony?
Do you resent those people with an ability to side-step life?

"What will it be? What will it be? The women churned the butter, drew the water, tended the fire. The Persians were threatening Athens. Total defeat or total victory. The victors would slit the throats of the wounded in the battlefield; they would advance on the city and force the gates. Rape for the women; death for the older men and the boys. The burning of the city. Babies smashed against the walls. Old women tormented and tortured for the pleasure of drunken louts. Idols smashed and the gods insulted. Did the Spartans arrive with vast numbers? Did the Marathon soldiers prevail? Tending the dinner; rocking the cradle; wondering and wondering what has transpired. If only a messenger would arrive and bring the word."

Harvie Heights - Banff - Lake Louise - Field - Leachoil - Golden - Blaeberry - Donald - Canyon Hot Springs - Revelstoke - Craigellachie - Malakwa - Sicumous - Canoe - Salmon Arm - Tappen - Balmoral - Blind Bay - Sorrento - Squilax - Chase - Shuswap - Pritchard - Monte Creek - Kamloops - Savona - Walhachin - Cache Creek - Boston Flats - Spences Bridge - Kanaka Bar - Keefers.

"As he approaches his one hundred and forty-second day of running across the vast expanse of Canada, Terry Fox will record his three thousand, three hundred and eighteenth mile."

"Well, nice to see you. Hope to see you again sometime. I run past here every week on my Saturday jog."

Running, running, running. Pain is getting worse. Twenty-six miles one day. Can't walk across the street the next. Pain is that force that in your mind you have to control. I think of other people when the pain gets really bad.
A group of cheerful people having a barbecue.
A beautiful reception at night in Terrace Bay. Telling them how I'm do-

ing. – Why I'm running. – How cancer can be beat. – About Greg as I try to keep the tears from my eyes. Cause it's not about me! I keep saying that everywhere I go! I keep telling people it's not me who should be noticed, but what I represent! I appreciate the attention, but not because I want to be rich or famous! I represent everyone who has ever had cancer in the past! Everyone who has cancer as we meet and talk tonight! And everyone who is going to get cancer in the future! We could have beaten it ten years ago! And we can beat it now! I want you to give so kids like Greg will have a future!

"Behind us, Terry Fox is romping in the cool waters of Jackfish Lake. Accompanying Terry in the hijinks in the water is Greg Scott, a ten year old amputee whom Terry first met in Hamilton, Ontario, a boy whom Terry says has inspired him on his run. The welcome respite comes after Terry's completion of twenty-six miles for the day."

"Can't seem to catch his breath while he's running."
"Should see those doctors and try to find out what's wrong."

Giving an interview for a documentary film.
A tortoise and a hare getting ready to race.
The Port Coquitlam Ravens basketball team.

"The Montreal River Hill was a big event for Terry. Just south of Wawa. Everybody along the route told him how hard it was going to be. Terry started talking about it as some kind of extra challenge. So we had a t-shirt made up about it for Terry to wear. The front said 'Montreal River Hill Here I Come'. The back said 'I've Got You Beat'. We weren't sure about the back. What was Terry gonna say? Maybe he'd think we were putting a curse on him by taking the hill for granted. You know Terry sometimes said that running on one leg was like running uphill would be for other people. So actually running up a hill must have been pretty strenuous for Terry with his artificial leg. So we come to the hill and he stops for a drink of water and says 'Here goes' and he just starts going up the hill slow and steady as if it was just like any other stretch of road. He stopped a few times, for breaks, but he kept up the pace despite the strain in his face and finally he stopped and said 'Nice to get that done.' He seemed to see it as a sign. There was a feeling that things would ease-up after that."

A group of kids diving from a dock.
A bulldozer scraping the topsoil into a pile.
A group of motorcycles cruising along a road.

A marathon a day - tracking me down - give it to you straight - cross a
threshold - one single painful devastating day - where the big ones go - rivalling

the himalayas - managing his life - whispered in the dark - rises up out of the midst.

The man whose son died of cancer. He and his wife invited us back to stay at their house. A hot shower and a home-cooked meal on a rainy day.

Greg and his dad who came from St. Catharines. Greg rode six miles beside me on his bike. Greg never lost his enthusiasm for life.

The welder who was watching the news on tv. It said I was having trouble with my artificial leg. He jumped right into his truck and came to help.

"If I concentrate on everything," the acolyte asked,
"Will everything in the world not seem the same?"

Running, running, running. From Terrace Bay to Shrieber.
A curly-haired smiling celebrity on every front-page.
So who's the real Terry Fox? I know there's people playing that game. Truth is – they're all the real Terry Fox. But I want to concentrate everyone's attention on only one – the Terry Fox who's running for cancer – who runs twenty-six miles every day – who's doing it for the kids – who's collecting all this money for cancer research – who's crossing Canada on one good leg – whose life is completely dedicated to the cause. Those other Terry Foxes – the one who starts the food fights – who eats french fries and burgers for lunch – who gets mad if the water isn't ready at every mile – who looks tired and distracted while you wait in line for an autograph or a cheerful chat – who's crying in pain with the van door closed while you wait for him to come out and say hello. That Terry Fox is me, but it's the one I keep to myself. What I do when I'm on the road – what I say when I'm on the road – the pain, the running, the message – the money collected to help the kids – that's the Terry Fox for everyone. What I do when I'm off the road – what I am when I'm off the road – that's the Terry Fox for me and the guys in the van.

"Television personnel, in reviewing footage of Terry Fox which has been recorded during his north-of-Superior run, have noted the presence of a very persistent cough in all of his interviews, giving rise to the speculation that all is not well concerning the state of Terry's health."

Enjoying the sunrise over Lake Superior.
Stopping to adjust the strap on my leg.

Kids donating their recess money.
Matching Christmas sweaters knitted by our grandma.
A country with six geological regions.

"I felt he was running for me. Specifically for me. Oh, he was running for every other Canadian – I know that – for every other person in the world, actually – but I felt that he was running especially for me. And I didn't have cancer – that's the thing. And I didn't go out to see him. Where I live is miles from anywhere. Only a few hundred live in my town. The joke around here is that if you run a few miles past our farm – our little spot on the road – you'll drop off the edge of the world. No, I'd seen him on TV as he ran across the country. And our local newspaper always gave him a lot of space. My means are limited, I couldn't travel, so I didn't get to see him. But I've always had a sense of all the agony in the world. How so many people seem to suffer from so many things. And here was this boy, from British Columbia, doing something about it. Raising money to try to alleviate some of the pain. And it made me feel a little less helpless. I didn't have cancer but he was running for me. He was doing it for all the people who live in pain. I felt he was running to carry a message from people like me."

Two freighters passing about a mile off-shore.
An old couple on rocking chairs on a porch.
A vegetable stand at the end of a country laneway.

"He's giving us everything he has."
"He hasn't kept an iota in reserve."

The day it all begins - talking earnestly in a phone booth - returning from the oracle - infiltrate and destroy - run past the pain - choose that story or no - thought it was just a scratch - a tortoise and a hare - told his story - make up the image.

The whole thing is such an adventure. And all of it is happening to me. People are calling me a hero, but as far as I'm concerned, I'm just Terry Fox.

I'm not disabled or handicapped. I'm a one-legged runner – nothing less and nothing more. I'm running to show that the impossible can be done.

People think I'm going through a nightmare. They think I'm going through hell. But my dream is coming true and that makes it worthwhile.

"The gods who were on your side were very persuasive.
They wrung a small concession from the group.
The gods decided that you will get to choose which leg."

Running, running, running. Rossport to Pays Plat. There's something about my stride that isn't right.

A runner slumped against a van at the side of a road.

It's not the artificial leg – it's something inside me. Something has shifted and I don't know what it is. I don't know what it is that's making things different. – The heat? – The hills? – The lack of sleep? Waking up exhausted. Barking at the others to leave me alone. Feeling weak and empty. Sulking and crying and pressing my chest. The heat and humidity are getting me down. Nearly fainted near Blind River as I was running. Had to stop and lie down for a while and then get up and run. But I'm not going to let it stop me. Pain is something you overcome. I've seen people in so much pain that my pain is nothing. In the cancer wards the pain is so strong it's like people are being tortured. So why shut down when I feel a little sore?

Freezing cold; pouring rain.
Did you think it would be this bad?

A man returning from an oracle.
Giving my mom and dad a hug as I leave BC.
Giving a speech of thanks about Doug.

Running freely.
A smooth groove.

"These collisions were the culminating events in the generation of a new super-continent, Pangea."

Sad to say that none of us
Gets to stay here very long.

What will you do if the cancer returns?
Would it strike you as grossly unfair?
Would you say you have more to live for than anyone else?

Lying on the bed and thinking of Greg. Glad his parents brought him to see me. Had a quiet talk with his dad. Greg's not as lucky as me. His cancer has come again. They found a spot of cancer on his lung.
A ten year old boy being towelled-off by his dad.
I've seen lonely stretches of highway and I've had thousands chanting my name. I've felt snow and sleet and hail and chilling rain. I've come up over a hill and seen some sights that have taken my breath away. I've laughed myself silly at hijinx and I've been doubled over in pain. I've cried on the phone with my parents and I've hugged them when they showed up for a surprise. I've looked cancer in the face – yellow eyes and blood-red fangs, late at night in the cancer ward – and said, Your victory over me will be pretty small. My victory

over you will be pretty big. I'm running for kids like Greg. As long as I can run I'll keep on running. As long as I can walk I'll keep on walking. If I have to crawl well then I'm going to crawl.

Chapter 15

Running, running, running. A stride, two hops, a stride. Heading for Thunder Bay.

A camera operator cleaning the lens of his camera.

Lots of people lining the road-side. Cheering me on. All the money goes to cancer. Every penny and every dime. If people don't hear about this it's a waste of time. People calling out as I pass them. – Way to go, Terry! – You can make it all the way! Camera crew waiting to film me. The One-legged Runner Who Can't Be Stopped. Shortness of breath. Ferocious pain. Will the pain stay the same or will it get worse? Wonder if one of these days they'll be filming my very last mile.

I believe in miracles.

Thinking about cancer and nothing else.
Dad, Mom, Fred, Terry, Darrell, Judith.
A teacher explaining to me how to talk to the kids.

I have to.

"If one were to glance at the globe, no doubt the most noticeable aspect of Canada would be its enormous size."

I have to believe that somewhere the hurting will stop.

Did you really believe that one day you would be fifty?

Did you imagine yourself out for a jog or a Saturday stroll?
Did you actually think that Phidippides would get to retire?

Running, running, running. Nipigon to Hurket. Can't seem to shake this cough. Always a dryness in my throat.
A man by the roadside coughing into a handkerchief.
Beautiful country north of Superior. Run for Cancer and Get to See Canada Coast-to-Coast. Not quite raining. A cloudy day. Lots of people lining the road. The radio stations are passing the word along. A steady rhythm. The kind I love. Gentle curves of the hills and valleys. Love to come back here when all this is over. Same for every part of the route. Waterfalls, rocks and trees. Taking Canada into my eyes, my ears and my lungs.

"We have word that Terry Fox, the one-legged runner, who recently celebrated his twenty-second birthday, has been forced to call a temporary halt to his Marathon of Hope, here, at this spot in Northern Ontario."

"This is the saddest thing in the world."
"How such terrible things can happen is hard to believe."

"With time and the concentrated efforts of the medical community, many people feel that the day might not be too far off when cancer – like polio or diphtheria – might well be one of those diseases which will be eradicated by one of those miracle breakthroughs which is always a possibility where modern medical science is concerned."

"I guess I'd have to say that I have two iconic images of the boy who was Terry Fox. One is running towards me. The grim look on his face and the curls damp with sweat. That awkwardly-graceful gait of his as he runs at the edge of the road. Always coming towards us with that look of quiet pain. Always getting bigger as he lopes his way along. The other is Terry Fox with his back to everyone. Running along at the edge of the road. The good leg and the artificial one working in harmony as he moves off into the mist. Getting smaller and further away with every stride. To me there will always be two of Terry Fox."

Sturgeon leaping high in a stream.
A sizzling frying pan on a wood stove.
A small girl showing the pages of a colouring book.

Just a kid with a dream - a thousand goals - various malignant neoplasms - looks over his shoulder - tell us the story - the voice inside - heard to make pronouncements - whose mom never recovered - living a normal life - feeling so awfully low.

I think it's all going to be okay. I passed the half-way mark not long ago. We're only eighteen miles from Thunder Bay.

I've learned to ignore what I have to ignore. Learned to concentrate on what I do best. I have the support of every Canadian along the way.

Soon I'll reach two-thirds of the journey. North of Superior's the toughest of all. After that every mile will seem like I'm running downhill.

The boy and his grandfather sat on the dock.
For hours, neither took his eyes off his line.

Running, running, running. Quimet to Pearl. Stopping and coughing along the roadside. No matter what I drink it's always there. Thought the air up here would make it go away.

A runner chugging a long cool drink of sparkling water.

Running, running, running. People lining along the route. – Keep going Terry! – Don't give up! – You can make it Terry! – We're all behind you! Good to hear. Good to hear. Even if I was alone, I would keep going anyway, but it's good to hear. I hear every word you say. I never respond when I'm running, but it's good to hear your voices. I hear every word you say and it means a lot. Hurts to run with this pain in my chest. When is this pain going to go away? I'll be here when this blister is gone. That's what I always say. It's what I hope I can say about all this pain.

"We have been given word that Terry is suffering from exhaustion from his long trek from Newfoundland, and that he is in need of a rest and medical tests. To date, he has run over half-way across Canada and is approaching the two-thirds mark as a means of raising donations for cancer research with an estimated two thousand, five hundred miles still to go."

Enjoying the morning as I run past a herd of cows.
Waking up a sleepy town with a loudhailer.

Dizziness, double-vision, fear of a heart attack.
People taking us home to their kitchen for chocolate cake.
A family with little kids in Winnipeg.

"Some say it was the running that brought back the cancer. Some say that it wasn't that at all. Even the doctors are divided. Some say it was caused by the accident in the little Cortina where he banged up his knee. Some say there was no connection – that he would have gotten cancer anyway. The funny thing is that all the time he was running Terry thought he was cancer-free. His biggest challenge was the risk of a heart attack. His heart would start to race and his eyes would go blurry and he'd feel dizzy for a while, then a drink of water or a short pause or sometimes a nap for twenty minutes and then he'd be right back out on the highway pounding along. Still – he didn't weigh the consequences – didn't calculate the cost. He ran a marathon a day in spite of the odds. He was willing to pay the price that had to be paid."

A cottage perched on a rocky cliff.
Snuggling under a blanket beside a fire.
Two men shingling a steep roof.

"He's living a dream that takes in all of Canada."
"Ocean to ocean; sea to sea; coast to coast."

What rage is hidden - something bad or dangerous - what is the point - scanning your brain - ailment needs a hero - what happens after - calling out your name - living in that zone - a drawer in the morgue - take myself to the limit.

The people who know me are the people I meet. In the classrooms and on the roads. Every one of them knows exactly what I am.

They read my face when I have a scowl. They read my face when I have a smile. They know every thought that I'm thinking as I run.

They know why I love my life. They know why I don't fear death. I run on one leg instead of walking on two.

The son never made any money.
For his father it had always been the same.
Each invested only in what he loved.

Running, running, running. Between Pearl and Thunder Bay. The pain in my chest is getting worse. Feels like a heart attack or something.
A runner pressing his hand against his chest.
What are the symptoms of a heart attack? – Shortness of breath. – Pain in the chest. – Numbness in the arm. What do you do with a mixture of symptoms? Maybe a little of every disease? Almost everything known to man is temporary. Almost everything known to man can be survived. There's only one word that I really don't want to hear. The camera crew gets their footage. The crew-members wave to me as I run past them. I think thanks but I don't take the energy to wave. Suddenly something hits me. Glad the camera-crew can't see me. I double over in pain. Stop running! Crawl into the van! Take me back to the room! There's something really wrong! It's not my ankle or my foot! It's something else!

"So vast is Canada that if there was a land-bridge across the Atlantic

Ocean, a runner would reach Europe in less time than it would take to run across the enormous expanse of Canada."

What have you packed into twenty-two years?
What have you done that is worth a whole life-time?
What seed have you planted in others that will continue to grow?

" 'A runner! Ho! A Runner! Open the gates! Let him inside!' The runner staggers in. Dusty and dirty; blood on his side. 'Get him some water!' Give him some room!' 'It is Phidippides, the runner!' 'Catch your breath! A sip of water! Try to tell us what you know! Is there any word from Marathon? Did the Spartans rush to our side? Did we engage with the Persians? What has transpired?' Phidippides lies in the dust. Tears of frustration in his eyes. The water wets his lips; he opens his mouth; he speaks the word. 'Rejoice, everyone! We conquer! Athens is saved!' 'Stand back; give him room; he needs some air.' 'Refill the bottle; give him drink; tend the wound in his side.' Hustle and bustle; an old man crying; relief and shouts of joy. Phidippides closes his eyes; his head is eased down to the dust. 'No need for water; no need for balm; no need to tend him now. This man has died.' "

Canyon Alpine - Boston Bar - Hells Gate - Spuzzum - Yale - Choate - Haig - Hope - Floods - Ruby Creek - Laidlaw - Popkum - Bridal Falls - Chilliwack - Kilgard - Abbotsford - Port Coquitlam - Burnaby - Vancouver - Victoria - Saanich - Longford - Colwood - Milnes Landing - Locke - Jordan River - Port Renfrew - Vancouver - Stanley Park.

"As of this moment, the facts are as follows: Terry Fox has spent sixty-six days in Ontario, for a total of one thousand four hundred and eighty-nine miles in this province. He has spent a total of one hundred and forty-three days running across Canada for a grand total – so far – of three thousand, three hundred and thirty-nine miles. When he gets back out on the road, he will have two thousand, five hundred miles left to run in order to reach his goal of dipping his leg in the Pacific Ocean in his home province of British Columbia."

Jogging through Stanley Park on a Saturday morning. My fiftieth birthday; a beautiful day. Who could believe?

Lying down in the motel room. Refusing to go to the hospital. Let the doctor come to me!
A crowd of people milling in a motel parking lot.
There's all those people outside. All those cameras. All those reporters. It'll be front-page news in the morning, but the only news they'll get is when I go back out and run. Huddling under a blanket. Ferocious pain like a fire in my

chest. The doctor arriving to check me over. The others huddling by the door. Somebody pushing the button on the silent TV.

"At this point, only eighteen miles from Thunder Bay, Ontario, Terry Fox has run an average of a marathon a day for one hundred and forty straight days. There is no record of this feat having been accomplished by any other runner, whether with one leg or with two."

"All we can do is be glad that it happened."
"Be grateful that we were blessed with Terry Fox."

Deciding that I will die before I quit.
Road hockey, baseball, basketball.
A person going for a jog on a Saturday morning.

"Terry was just like a little kid. He was romping around with Greg in the shallow water. They left their artificial legs behind on the bank. Greg and I flew up and surprised him. The others asked for us to come. They said that Terry was getting down and that he often talked of Greg and that he sometimes said that he wished that Greg could have ridden his bike across Canada alongside Terry. Terry met so many people and yet he felt a bond with Greg. So when we were asked I was really happy for Greg because he always talked of Terry and we always watched for Terry on the news. So as I was watching them laugh and shout and spray each other and dive in the water, I was wondering whether to tell my secret or not. Greg had been really good – about as cheerful as he could be – but he realized that he didn't have long to go. I sensed that Terry would want to know, so when the others were busy drying off, I motioned Terry aside and told him the news. Greg's cancer had returned. There wasn't a lot to say. Each of us knew what the other was thinking. It was something I needed to share. I just couldn't keep it inside. I needed to draw on the bond that Terry had with Greg."

A car with camping gear strapped on top.
A middle-aged man out for a morning jog.
A class of school-kids listening eagerly.

The flame which burns within you - twice the mind - a pair of shorts, a t-shirt and a single sock - knows everybody's name - osteogenic sarcoma - charges against you- what it was to be alive - brimming with health - it needs a process - knock out a plough horse.

It was the people who came to mean the run for me. Something from every person I talked to kept me going. They would cry sometimes when they told me why they were there.

People whose fathers were dying of cancer. People whose mothers were getting treatment. People who came from a cancer ward to see me run by.

I wish I had more time to talk to people. I have to break off every conversation to get back to my run. Someday, I'd like to take the train clear across Canada and just shoot the breeze with people at every stop.

"If you concentrate your focus on everything," the guru replied,
"You will be everything and everything will be you."

With the doctor in the hotel room. His face looks pretty grim.
An older man and a younger man face to face.
Checking everything I have. Tapping and probing and listening. Coughing and breathing deep when he asks me to. Wanting to know my medical history. Answering his questions as best I can. Him sitting back and me leaning forward. – It seems to be the lung. – Either an infection in the lung, or perhaps, the lung has collapsed. – I just can't tell anything further without some tests. I don't think I know more than he does, but I think I know what's the matter – and I think that he knows too. He's probably wondering who to report to instead of me. Asking them all to clear out of the room. Looking the doctor in the eye. The doctor looking right back at me. He waits for me to speak first. Thank you for coming, Doctor. Might as well get to the point. – Do you think it's cancer?

"Although we have been told that Terry Fox is taking a short break for medical purposes, we do not have any word, as yet, as to when he will be able to resume his run. His parents are flying in from Vancouver. Apparently Terry will speak to the media very soon."

Running to the next driveway or mailbox.
Running to the next telephone pole or crossroad.

A jug of Atlantic seawater in the van.
One mile, one corner, one sign, one more bend.
A serious disease caused by cells which are not normal.

"I was standing beside the highway. A cup of water in my hand. I was waiting for my brother. I had tears in my eyes and I knew it wasn't the wind. I had let my brother down. Just idle chatter to the media. 'Easy for Terry.' 'All he has to do is run.' 'It isn't easy serving Terry.' 'We do the work and all he does is complain'. Once you've talked to the media you're dead. They can twist it, distort it, turn it upside down. Or they can just print it as you said it and when you read it you're really stunned. Suddenly you're reading your own words with another person's eyes. Anyway, I wiped the tears away and held out the drink – but I didn't want to have to look Terry in the eye. I thought he might run right on past me or slap the cup from my hand, like he does those times when he's really, really mad. Anyway – Terry stopped running and gave me a silent hug."

Pine trees looming over the ribbon of road.
Sitting outside and talking under the stars.
A sunset slowly fading on Lake Superior.

"It's the kids who understand him more than anyone."
"They sing a song thanking God for Terry Fox."

To set an example - half as many socks - just how threatened - sense of a barrier - meaning behind the run - expect to be able to slay - become what people see - some days beautiful, some days brutal - time for my future - make the pain go away.

After Ontario, it will all be downhill. Pretty soon, I'll be two-thirds of the way. I can run all the way to Vancouver in my sleep.

I'll come running up to the ocean. I'll wade in the water and soak my leg. Atlantic to Pacific – every mile!

I'll keep visiting the cancer wards. Tons of scientists will work on research. Someday, when I visit those wards, there'll be no one there!

The runner thought and thought and thought.
At last he gave his answer to the gods.
"I only need one leg when I am running.
Let my good leg be the one that strikes the ground."

Running, running, running. A stride, two hops and a stride. This pain is getting ferocious. I'm running bent over in pain.

A runner getting smaller as he runs in the distance.

I didn't want to see that doctor. I knew it wouldn't be good news. Might have been better not to know. Now I've got cancer in my lungs. So it isn't just the knee anymore. He wants me to fly back home and get treatment. Why would I want to do that? Coughing – pain in my chest – blood on my stump. Nothing has stopped me so far. Who says you can't run with cancer? I've been doing it for three thousand miles. Sure, I might die of cancer, but my spirit will never die. People will know that I always kept trying. They'll know that I gave it my best.

Numbing cold; biting wind.
What's the point of all this pain?

Running with malignant neoplasms.
A tree about to fall in an ancient forest.

A tiny Cortina banging into the back of a truck.

Worst is behind you.
All downhill.

"To cross Canada today is to undergo a journey through a series of end-lessly-unfolding vistas of our primeval heritage of water, land and sky."

Good that others will be here to know
The sunrise and the song.

Why has your running affected so many people?
Have you had a fair return on all that pain?
Why do you say that you are just plain Terry Fox?

Running, running, running. Eighteen miles to Thunder Bay. What's pain if you ignore it? What's pain if you don't call it pain?
A runner getting bigger as he comes into sight.
The doctor was blunt. I asked him to be. Still, it hurt when he told me the truth. I didn't know what to do, so here I am running. It's the only thing I can think of. The pain in my chest is getting ferocious. Every mile could be my last mile. Still, it's all downhill to Vancouver. Don't want to let everyone down. Gotta keep running, running, running. I'll keep on running while I can. Eighteen miles to Thunder Bay. Two thousand miles to Vancouver. Twenty-six miles a day – one day at a time. If there's any way I can finish it, I will.

Three Books

Terry Fox: Somewhere the Hurting Must Stop – a novel
    A one-legged boy, Terry Fox, sets himself the task of running a marathon a day across the length of Canada, the second-largest country in the world, in aid of cancer research, because the children are crying with pain in the cancer wards and somewhere the hurting must stop.

The Making of the Somewhere the Hurting Must Stop – a reflective journal
    This journal records my reflections on the process of the crafting of the novel as it evolved through the stages of planning, writing, editing and polishing. It constitutes an effort to be as conscious as possible of the process whereby the single idea that suggested the topic of the novel was expanded into a complex work of art. Topics range from the nuts and bolts of novel-building to the nature of the novel as an art-form.

Planning Somewhere the Hurting Must Stop – a planning notebook
    During the writing of the novel, I kept a hand-written notebook which records the day-by-day development of the novel as it found its shape and style. The notebook – now in print form – reveals how a vast cluster of thoughts was sifted, selected, structured and polished into novel-form.

The Project
    Together, this novel, journal and notebook comprise the nineteenth installment in an on-going novel-writing project in which I am exploring the concept of form and meaning in the novel, and of the novel as a form of expression in the 21st Century. All of the published journals and notebooks are available for free download at www.johnpassfield.ca.

About the Author

John Passfield was born in St. Thomas, Ontario, Canada, and continues to reside in Southern Ontario, near Cayuga, with his family. He is interested in exploring the development of the novel as an art-form, and has written over twenty novels, twenty planning notebooks and twenty journals in his search for a form for the poetic novel of our time.

Novels by John Passfield

Grave Song
The Agony of Robert Chisholm

Jumbo
P. T. Barnum's Greatest Creation

Pinafore Park
The Swan Boat Incident

Water Lane
The Pilgrimage of Christopher Marlowe

Rain of Fire
The Ordeal of Conductor Spettigue

Victoria Day
The Fabric of the Community

The Wright Brothers
Flight is Possible

Leni Riefenstahl
The Valley of the Shadow

Babe Ruth
Out of the Park

Raskolnikov
Murder with an Axe

Sergei Eisenstein
Death Day

Albert Einstein
Wonder

Geoffrey Chaucer
Canterbury Bound

Ospringe
A Visit with Grandad

Pompeii
Vesuvius Dominus

Beethoven
The Ninth Immersion

Job
The Cornerstone of the Universe

Bethune
The Only Person Alive in the World

Terry Fox
Somewhere the Hurting Must Stop

Lord and Lady Macbeth
Full of Scorpions Is My Mind

Cyril Passfield
Out West

See www.johnpassfield.ca for publishing information.

In Search of Form and Meaning: Journals by John Passfield

Each journal is a day-by-day record of the complex process that a writer undergoes while crafting a work of art. It records the largest decisions, of structure and theme, and the smallest decisions, such as the choice of one word over another, and the constant interaction between the two. Each journal is a record of a writer's reflection on the craft of novel-writing.

The Making of Grave Song

The Making of Jumbo

The Making of Pinafore Park

The Making of Water Lane

The Making of Rain of Fire

The Making of Victoria Day

The Making of Flight is Possible

The Making of The Valley of the Shadow

The Making of Out of the Park

The Making of Murder with an Axe

The Making of Death Day

The Making of Wonder

The Making of Canterbury Bound

The Making of Ospringe

The Making of Vesuvius Dominus

The Making of The Ninth Immersion

The Making of The Cornerstone of the Universe

The Making of The Only Person Alive in the World

The Making of Somewhere the Hurting Must Stop

The Making of Full of Scorpions Is My Mind

The Making of Out West

See www.johnpassfield.ca for publishing information.

The Novel as an Art-Form:
Planning Notebooks by John Passfield

Each planning notebook is a printed version of the hand-written notebook which records the planning, writing, editing and polishing of each novel. Each notebook is an attempt to record, understand, and organize the vast cluster of thoughts which occur as one grapples with the various levels of organization which a clear yet complex work of art demands.

Planning Grave Song

Planning Jumbo

Planning Pinafore Park

Planning Water Lane

Planning Rain of Fire

Planning Victoria Day

Planning Flight is Possible

Planning The Valley of the Shadow

Planning Out of the Park

Planning Murder with an Axe

Planning Death Day

Planning Wonder

Planning Canterbury Bound

Planning Ospringe

Planning Vesuvius Dominus

Planning The Ninth Immersion

Planning The Cornerstone of the Universe

Planning The Only Person Alive in the World

Planning Somewhere the Hurting Must Stop

Planning Full of Scorpions Is My Mind

Planning Out West

See www.johnpassfield.ca for publishing information.